TOCCOA'S ECHOES

By M. C. VAUGHN

SPLINTERED INFINITY PRESS, LLC.
SAVANNAH, GA., US

This novel is a work of fiction. Any resemblance between the characters in this novel and actual persons is purely unintentional and coincidental.

Acknowledgements:
Thank you again to my family and friends for your continued support and encouragement. As always, a special thank-you to Danny Simanjaya for his wonderful cover art; hope you and your Mrs. can make it back to Savannah soon!

This book is in memory of, and dedicated to, the thirty-nine persons who lost their lives in the flood stemming from the failure of the Kelly Barnes Dam in Toccoa Falls, Georgia on November 6, 1977:

Karen Anderson
Rebecca Anderson
William L. Ehrensberger
Robert Ehrensberger
Kenny Ehrensberger
Mary Jo Ginther
Nancy Ginther
Tracy Ginther
Tiep Harner
Christopher Kemp
Dirksen Metzger
Jeremiah Moore
Carol Pepsny
Bonnie Pepsny
Monroe J. Rupp
Melissa Sproull
Joanna Sproull
Jaimee Veer
Paul I. Williams
Deborah Woerner

Joseph Anderson
Gerald Brittin
Peggy Ann Ehrensberger
Kristen Ehrensberger
David Fledderjohann
Brenda Ginther
Rhonda Ginther
Cary E. Hanna
Robbie Harner
Cassandra Metzger
Ruth Moore
Edward E. Pepsny
Paul Pepsny
Eloise J. Pinney
Jerry Sproull
Jocelyn Sproull
Richard J. Swires
Mary N. Williams
Betty Jean Woerner

TOCCOA'S ECHOES

IN MEMORIAM

From the McDowell Mills Herald:

ABBOTT, ALBERT JOHN, Specialist 2nd Class, U.S. Army Air Forces (Ret.) – born June 3, 1917, Jackson Creek, Ga; passed away Tuesday, November 26, 1957 at his home in McDowell Mills. Mr. Abbott served stateside as a mechanic and instructor in the Army Air Corps during the Second World War, and moved with his wife to McDowell Mills from Jackson Creek in 1946. He is survived by his wife, the former Helena Rutledge; brother, Joseph Abbott of Jackson Creek; sister, Jane Abbott Sawyer, her husband, Hubert, and their son Edward Hubert Sawyer, of Toccoa, Georgia. Mr. Abbott was preceded in death by his father, Hubert Abbott, and his mother, Jane Chandler Abbott, both of Jackson Creek. A funeral service will be held at First New Jerusalem Methodist Church on Friday, November 29 at 2pm, with interment to follow.

From the Toccoa Star-Echo:

SAWYER, EDWARD HUBERT – born July 31, 1949, Toccoa, Ga.; passed away Sunday, November 6, 1977 in Toccoa Falls, in the flood following the failure of the Kelly Barnes dam. Edward and his wife, the late Roberta Brown Sawyer, were graduates of Stephens County High School. Edward was employed at Toccoa Falls College. He is survived by his mother, Jane Abbott Sawyer, and his aunt, Helena Abbott, both of Toccoa, and an infant daughter, Roberta Jane Sawyer. Funeral services to be announced.

SAWYER, ROBERTA BROWN – born October 7, 1950, Canon, Ga; passed away Sunday, November 6, 1977 in Toccoa Falls, in the flood following the failure of the Kelly Barnes dam. Roberta and her husband, the late Edward Hubert Sawyer, were graduates of Stephens County High School; Edward was employed at Toccoa Falls College. She is survived by her mother-in law, Jane Abbott Sawyer, his aunt Helena Abbott, both of Toccoa, and an infant daughter, Roberta Jane Sawyer. Funeral services to be announced.

CHAPTER ONE

"YOU REALLY WANT to go to Lavonia? That's a long way from here."

Stephanie gave me that look she always did whenever I suggested anything that might get in the way of what she wanted. It was a cute look, but it was also one of the reasons she and I stopped dating the previous year, and anyway, she and Steve were officially together – so as far as I was concerned, how cute she looked didn't matter.

"It's over two hours away. Taking the interstate isn't any faster than going through Athens, because it takes us so far out of the way." Stephanie pouted a bit. "But we know who she is, and where she is now. Helena Abbott. She's at the New Star Assisted Living Facility, in Lavonia. We really ought to go there and find out what we can."

"I understand," I answered. "But even if we learn something, Mr. Abbott never pays any attention to us. He doesn't even argue with the other ghosts about which side of the graveyard is better."

"Well, he's on the side where all the weird stories are buried," Stephanie answered. I gave her a dark look.

"The side where all the weird stories everyone *knows about*, you mean. I'll bet the old families on the church side are just as messed up. They're probably even worse, since they were the ones who ran everything for years. They were the ones sweeping everything under the rug. Six feet under, to be exact."

"*Chad Campbell!*" she hissed at me. My voice had gotten a little loud for the library, which would have gotten us in trouble if anyone else besides Miss Roberts, the librarian, had been there. Even just a couple of months ago, I would have been told – severely – to modulate my tone, but Miss Roberts' attitude toward us had changed greatly after we uncovered the true story of what had happened to her high school friend, Sarah Beckwith.

"OK, OK," I said more quietly. Stephanie looked less than mollified, but after a glance toward Miss Roberts' door, she sighed.

"I wish Steve was here," she said.

"So do I," I answered her. "I'll call him tonight and see whether he wants in on this trip."

"No, I'll call him," Stephanie replied. "If he's not sure he wants to go, I can persuade him."

"Yeah. 'Persuade,'" I said sardonically. She just grinned at me, and as she did, I saw Miss Roberts emerge from the door behind her. She looked quizzically at us.

"Did you find anything new?" she asked.

"We did," I replied. "One of the – the people in the New Jerusalem cemetery was a man named Albert Abbott. We used his obituary to track down his sister, and we found his wife, too. They live up in North Georgia, near Lake Hartwell. We were going to ask whether there is a city map of Lavonia anywhere in the library."

Miss Roberts gave us a funny look. "Albert Abbott? Died in the late nineteen-fifties?" she asked.

"That's the one," Stephanie answered. The librarian's eyebrows arched.

"There were a lot of odd stories surrounding the Abbotts," she said. "His death was just about as mysterious as Sarah Beckwith's was, and his wife – Helena, I think – left McDowell Mills the day after his funeral. To my knowledge, she never came back." She paused. "Where did you say she is now?"

"His sister used to live in Toccoa, in the northeast corner of the state. She worked at the college there," I replied. "As far as I know, she's still there, though she's retired now. After we checked the obituary, and found her in an old directory at the college, Stephanie wrote to her. She wrote back and told us where Helena is. She's in a nursing home in Lavonia. The obituary said they have a nephew there, too, but we don't know where he is."

Miss Roberts blinked. "I'd forgotten her name, until you just said it," she said. "Helena Abbott. She and her husband were just typical folks, living just outside town towards New Jerusalem, until the fire." She paused, looking at us thoughtfully. "You know, I've wanted to go to Lavonia for some time. There's a library there that was funded by Andrew Carnegie, some eighty years ago. He paid for hundreds of libraries all over the country, even in little out-of-the-way places like Lavonia. I think it might be time for me to make that trip."

Stephanie and I glanced at each other. Being still in high school, we knew the biggest obstacle to visiting Helena would be getting our parents' permission. When Miss Roberts spoke again, she clearly had had the same thought.

"Your parents would be more likely to let you go to Lavonia if I come with you. I assume you wouldn't mind riding with me?" It wasn't really a question, but truthfully, that didn't matter.

"It would be a big help to us," Stephanie said, before I could get a word in. "You're right, our parents probably would let us go as far as Athens, but Lavonia is almost twice that far." I nodded in surprised agreement, and Miss Roberts favored us with a rare smile.

"Have your parents contact me, and we can go this weekend. Be here at eight on Sunday morning. That's the only time I can go, since this library's closed on Sundays for the summer." She paused. "I'll contact the librarian in Lavonia and see whether I can persuade them to let me tour the place off-hours."   Without waiting for a response, she turned and walked back to her office. Stephanie whistled softly under her breath as the door closed.

"If I hadn't just seen that, I would never have believed it," I said.

"Me either," Stephanie answered. "I'll call Steve when I get home."

She looked really excited, and I knew I was, as well. "You think we can help them?"

"The Abbotts? Maybe." She seemed less enthusiastic after I asked. "I just hope there isn't something awful that came between them. Sarah's story was terrible enough, but it had a good ending."

"Exactly." I felt the same sense of caution that clearly had affected her. "If it was bad enough, or enough of the wrong people knew, it would explain why Albert never seems to acknowledge anyone."

"I'd guess there was a lot of whispering about what might have happened to him," Stephanie said. "He died in a house fire, and his wife didn't stay around afterward. People in this town gossip a lot more about a lot less."

"True." I thought for a moment. "I wonder whether Miss Mollie would know anything about it. After all, Albert did die around the time her shop opened. At the least, she's probably heard *something*."

Stephanie nodded, then looked at the clock. "Crap. I have to go. My aunt and uncle are coming to visit tomorrow and my mom wants me to help make sure the house is in order."

"OK." I knew better than to ask her to wait any longer; Stephanie typically wanted what she wanted, when she wanted it. Steve Smith was the only person I'd ever seen who had ever had any effect on that part of her personality.

We gathered our notebooks, packed them in our bookbags – which were much lighter than usual, seeing as it was summer – and made out way to the parking lot and my truck. I knew I was low on gas, but I also knew Stephanie would want to go home first. Even so, I gave her a glance as I fired up the truck and backed it out of my space, turning onto Highway 255 and driving south, back toward town, and turning onto Ferry Street. She lived less than a mile away, in one of the neighborhoods that had been built in the sixties between the town square and the railroad tracks. The needle on my fuel gauge was still slightly above the "E," and I breathed a sigh of relief. I still had about ten miles in the tank.

"You want me to go ask Miss Mollie about the Abbotts?" I asked before I'd really thought about what I was saying. Stephanie frowned.

"It's usually best if we go together," she replied. "One of us might catch something that the other would miss."

It wasn't hard to determine who "one" and "the other" were in that scenario, but I let it pass. Stephanie was Stephanie. I steered the truck onto Candler Street and passed three houses before turning left into her driveway. As she got out, she looked at me, and I guess I must have appeared a little annoyed.

"I'm sorry," she said. "But really, the more of us there are talking with Miss Mollie, the better a chance we have of understanding everything. It's just as true of me as it is of you."

I smiled in reply. "I know. I get it," I answered.

She studied me for a moment, then smiled back. "All right, then," she said, and closed the door, walking through the garage and into her house. I glanced behind me to make sure I wasn't going to hit anything, and got back out onto Candler Street, going back the way I came, and hoping that the fuel gauge wasn't lying to me.

IT WAS AFTER DARK when Stephanie called me.

"I talked to Steve," she said. "He said he'd meet us here and that we could ride together up to Lavonia on Sunday. He's going to run it past his parents, but he thinks they'll let him go."

"Good. Have you told Joey and Lori yet?"

"Not yet," Stephanie answered. "I'm worried that if too many of us show up at the nursing home, it might intimidate Helena, and we don't want that. Can you tell them for me?"

I thought about that for a minute. "I guess so," I replied. I didn't want to say so, but I thought that might be the best way to handle it. Stephanie meant well, but she could sometimes say things the wrong way. Again, the only person she seemed to avoid irritating at one point or other was Steve, and secretly, I suspected that she was really deeply in love with him, and that made her so nervous that she would think before speaking when he was around.

"OK – thanks," she said. "Go ahead and call Joey and tell him what's up."

"All right. See you Saturday," she said, and hung up before I could reply. That was also typical of Stephanie. Saying goodbye had been awkward for us, ever since we stopped dating and agreed to just be friends.

I hit the reset on the phone and dialed Joey. Thankfully, he answered the phone; Joey's father was a jerk, one of the McDowell Mills jocks from the previous generation who had finished school with little education, no prospects, and a bad knee that excluded him from military service, forcing him to work the assembly line in the local appliance factory – a factory that, by 1993, was barely clinging to life. I always felt sorry for him for having to deal with his dad, but Joey had always seemed able to handle the situation.

"Hey, we think we found out some stuff about Albert Abbott," I told him.

His voice came back up the line. "Lori told me you guys were trying to find out about him. He's another McDowell Mills Special, definitely."

"Oh yeah," I replied. "Stephanie tracked down his wife. After she left, she moved to Toccoa – that's way up in the northwest corner of the state. She lives in a nursing home now in a town called Lavonia. Funny thing is, Miss Roberts wants to go there too. She says there's something about the library there, and that she wants to go see it this Sunday."

"Wow. That'll make it easier for you to convince your folks to let you go." Joey's voice dropped. "I have to mow the yard and weed my mom's flowerbeds this weekend, so I can't, and Lori and I were going to go to a movie that afternoon anyway."

"OK." I sighed with relief. "Stephanie was worried that if too many of us came, it might intimidate Helena – Albert's wife – so she suggested that just she and Steve and I would go. I hope that's not a problem."

"No problem. Let me know what you find out." He was silent for a minute. "My dad just got home. I'd better go."

"I hear you. I'll check with you on Monday. Bye." After Joey's answering goodbye, I hung up, already wondering whether anything would come of this weekend trip – and also remembering that I needed to ask my parents whether I could go, though I wasn't worried that they wouldn't let me. Our school's math team had traveled to Americus and to Augusta during the previous school year, and both of those trips had been long enough that we had had to stay in a hotel overnight.

I left my bedroom and went into the kitchen. Mom was clearing up after dinner, and looked over at me. "Can you load these in the dishwasher?" she asked.

"Sure." I knew my mom hated doing dishes, so I figured any help would make her more likely to agree to the trip. I opened the dishwasher to discover that the previous load hadn't been put away. She had made a similar calculation to mine.

Smiling ruefully, I unloaded the dishwasher and put everything away without a word, then began reloading it. Mom had finished clearing up the dishes and flatware and stacked it all in the right side of the sink for me to load. A few minutes later, everything was loaded and I had started the dishwasher again.

Mom had moved to the living room sofa by that time. Dad was already in his recliner, and they were watching a Clint Eastwood movie. Dad loved Dirty Harry. I didn't care for those movies that much, not because they were bad – they weren't – but the plots and scripts always glorified the lead character, regardless of his flaws. Most of those films were made in the 1970s, and hadn't aged very well.

After waiting a few minutes, I asked my mom: "Stephanie and Steve and I want to go up to a town called Lavonia this weekend. Miss Roberts agreed to drive us up, since she wants to visit the library there." Mom was a reader – she was where I got it from – and she knew Miss Roberts fairly well, as she had been the only librarian in town since the time she was in school.

Mom looked at me, and I could tell she wasn't sure about my request. "Why would you need to go there?" she asked.

"It's for the MMHS Historical Society," I answered. "We learned about someone who died in a house fire on the 1950s, a man named Albert Abbott. His wife left McDowell Mills right after his funeral, and moved to Toccoa. She still lives there."

"I don't know that that's a good idea," she answered. "If she left that quickly, she might not want to talk about what happened."

"That's what we thought, too, at first," I said. "But we found out that she lived with Mr. Abbott's sister for years, even after the sister married. So she might have left because that was the only family she had."

My mom thought about that. "Are you sure you want to go asking someone who lost her husband about how he died?"

"Yes," I answered emphatically. "Everything about it was hushed up, but one of the things the Society has figured out has to do with the First New Jerusalem graveyard. Until the 1970's, the only people they buried across the highway from the church were non-members and people who died after a scandal. Albert Abbott got buried out there in 1957, so it fits. We'd like to find out the real story."

Mom considered again. She was from one of the second-line old families, people who weren't the big movers and shakers in McDowell Mills, but rather the tradesmen and entrepreneurs who had managed to succeed in spite of the town fathers. Some of those families had streets named after them, in some of the less savory parts of town; Robbins Street, which was in a poor neighborhood on the other side of the tracks from Candler Street, had been named for my mom's grandfather, Michael Robbins, back in the 1930s. My great-grandfather had rebuilt the rail terminal in McDowell Mills around 1922, and had been rewarded by having one of the worst streets in town named after him. Fittingly, the building was razed in the 1970s, since the passenger rail service had ended after the Second World War.

"All right. As long as you have Miss Roberts along." Mom's assent broke my reverie. "What time do you plan on leaving?"

"Sunday morning, early," I answered. "We're going to go up to Tuckerton to pick up Steve, and then the four of us will be going up from there. It'll be about two-and-a-half hours each way."

"And you're just going to talk to this man's wife, Mrs. Abbott?" she asked pointedly.

"We'd like to interview his sister, too," I answered. "She might have some different insights about him."

Mom thought about that for a few seconds, then nodded. "All right. But try to be back no later than seven or eight on Sunday. I don't want to be worried about you all driving that far at night."

"OK. Mom. Thanks," I answered. "Let me call Steve and let him know we're on for Sunday."

She nodded and turned her attention back to the movie. I knew she'd seen it before, but my dad liked it, so she just went along. They were like that with a lot of things.

I went back into the kitchen and dialed Steve. Evidently he'd been waiting on me to call, since he picked it up before the first ring had finished.

"Hey Steve. My folks are fine with us going up on Sunday," I told him.

"Great," he answered. "Once school starts, it's going to be a lot harder for us to get together." He paused. "I was telling my folks about this, and they told me something that we might want to look into while we're up there."

"Really?" I was surprised. "How would they know anyone way up there?"

"Not any*one*," he replied. "Any*thing*. There's a community college up there – Toccoa Falls Bible College – that was hit by a flood after a dam broke, back in the 1970s. It happened at night, so no one knew it was coming, and it killed a *lot* of people." He paused. "We might want to see if there's anywhere up there where ghosts congregate."

I thought about that for a moment. "Congregate. Interesting word choice for a Bible college," I said, then added, "but that might not be a bad idea. New Jerusalem is at a church, even if the ghosts aren't all members or even believers."

"And Toccoa Falls has at least one dark place in its history," Steve added. "Kind of like the train wreck in McDowell Mills in 1911. And that's without all the Civil War and segregation stuff that went on for a hundred years, or the slavery period before that, or the native Americans being forced out of Georgia. I'll try to find out more, but there's reason to think that it could be the kind of place with a lot of bad, unfinished stories."

I had to agree. "You look for that on your end. We still have to try to reach Mr. Abbott, and he always ignores us."

"I thought Stephanie might be the right person to ask him," Steve said. "If we tell him we know about Helena, that might be enough to get his attention. He doesn't seem like Sarah –

she was looking for someone. Mr. Abbott would know his wife left and never came back, so he isn't waiting on anyone. He's just stuck here. Stephanie might have a better chance of making him hear us."

"OK. Yeah, I think you're right." I thought for a few moments. "Why don't we get together on Tuesday, maybe get some burgers, and then head out to the cemetery? We've only been once since summer started."

"That's true." Steve paused. "I know that's kind of my fault, since Stephanie and I are together. She usually wants to go someplace that isn't in McDowell Mills."

"We all want that," I answered. "But they're finally building a movie theater here, and a couple of chain restaurants are being built on the interstate. Cleve's isn't terrible, but I could really go for a Waffle Grille." I paused. "Too bad it's not open yet."

"I'm just surprised it took them that long to get tired of the same thing every day," Steve pointed out. "It took some new people moving in for everyone to see how stodgy that place is."

"That's a good word for it," I answered. "See you Tuesday, then. Say six o'clock, we meet at Cleve's?"

"Sure. See you then," he answered, and hung up.

CHAPTER TWO

THAT TUESDAY, I picked up Stephanie just before six and drove over to Cleve's. Steve usually drove her home, but with the distance he had to drive to get from Tuckerton, I would sometimes pick her up in case he got behind a wreck on the way.

We pulled into the diner and parked. Even a year before, the place would have been full, but the trickle of new businesses elsewhere in the county had already started to whittle away at its customer base. I realized that when there were a few more choices in town, Cleve's would have to adapt, or the place would go by the wayside.

Evidently, Stephanie was thinking the same thing. "I thought it would be more crowded," she said. "Well, unless Steve's late, that'll be less of a wait for us."

We went inside, and for the first time that I could remember, we were able to get a table right away. It was so unusual that for a moment, we were both tongue-tied. Stephanie was watching the window, waiting for Steve's truck to appear.

"Steve and I thought you should be the one to try to tell Mr. Abbott about Helena," I heard myself say. That got her attention.

"Why me?" she asked. "Steve's the one who usually gets the ghosts to listen."

"Not really," I replied. "Sarah was waiting for Steve's uncle, and Steve looked just like him. And Tommy – Tommy talked to everyone. Steve just happened to be the one who saw where his ball was."

"I guess that's true," she replied doubtfully. "But why do you think I'd do better talking to Mr. Abbott? He never listens to any of us."

"None of us knew about his wife, except that she left," I answered. "He might listen if someone knew more, and told him so. I just think he would be more likely to listen to a girl, especially if there was something bad about what happened. He might warn you off, if it was a really dark story, but if Steve or I tried to tell him, he might not care one way or another."

"But we're still just guessing," Stephanie protested. "I'm not sure whether we should even tell him yet."

"He may not even know where she is," I argued back, but Stephanie had been distracted by the arrival of Steve's elderly truck. He had had it repainted in metallic-flake midnight blue, and it really looked sharp. It was hard to believe that vehicle had once been as unpleasant, if not outright nasty, as its former owner. I wondered whether the truck's restoration went hand-in-hand with Fred's redemption.

I glanced toward Stephanie as Steve got out. She watched him in a way I'd never seen her look with anyone else. When she and I had dated, I always got the feeling that she was the center of her own little universe, and everything else revolved around her. It was one reason we had agreed to be friends, instead of dating seriously. With Steve, it was as though she was the one in his orbit, but to his great credit, they really seemed to circle each other, like a binary star.

Steve came into the diner, looked around momentarily, and spied us. A big smile crossed his face, and he was soon seated next to Stephanie, who snuggled close to him as he put his arm around her. "Hi, guys!" he said.

"Hey," I replied. "Stephanie and I were just talking about how to get Mr. Abbott to listen to us."

"Yeah." He glanced down at her, squeezing her gently with his arm. "I think Chad's right about this. You guys know more about his wife than I do, so it should be one of you, and I know that I'd prefer talking to a girl."

Stephanie took a swipe at his chest that was mostly playful, but I sensed that she was just slightly worried by the prospect. Trying to reassure her, I said, "We should decide exactly what to tell Mr. Abbott before we go to the graveyard. That way you'll already have some idea of what you want to say, and you won't be as nervous about approaching him."

"Y'all know what you want?" interjected an adult, female voice. We looked up, startled, to see a graying, matronly waitress wearing a pink uniform and a slightly disapproving expression. She held a pen and ordering pad, and – apparently – a distrustful attitude toward younger customers. Her name tag read "TINA."

"Sorry, uh – Tina," I answered quickly. "We didn't mean to be rude."

"This all on one check, or are you separate?" Tina asked.

"I got it," Steve said, before I could answer. I started to protest, but Steve gave me a look that told me to wait, so I let it go. "I'll just have the burger and fries. No onions, if you could, please. And a lemonade," he continued. Cleve's never cleaned its soft-drink machines, but they made great lemonade, so that was what most people ordered.

Tina jotted this down, silently, before looking toward Stephanie. "What's the special today?" she asked.

"Meat loaf and gravy with cabbage," Tina replied. Her stare spoke volumes about what to expect.

"I'll have what he's having, then," she said, looking toward Steve. Tina nodded again.

"I'll have a BLT," I said. "Fries with it, please. And lemonade."

"Thank you," Steve said, as Tina sauntered away. As she called out the order to the cooks, Steve smiled again. "You guys have to save more for college than I do. It turned out Fred left me some money, so I can use what I make from work to have a little more fun. Or –" he pointed out the window – "to fix up the truck."

"It looks amazing," I observed. "I wouldn't have thought you could have gotten it in shape like that."

"I named her Sarah," he replied, grinning.

Tina returned to our table, carrying three large, clear plastic cups of lemonade, and looked around at the three of us. "I'll have your plates for you in just a minute." Before we could respond, she left again.

"Guys, I still don't know what I should say," Stephanie said, a bit plaintively. "And if I say the wrong thing, we might never get Mr. Abbott to listen."

Steve thought about that for a moment, and an odd look crossed his face. "Maybe we're going about this all wrong," he said. Stephanie and I both looked quizzically at him.

"From what you've told me, whenever someone's tried to get his attention, they were talking at him, or trying to get him to acknowledge something," he said. "What if he's always had something that he needs to say, but we've never acted like we care about what he thinks?"

"What do you mean?" Stephanie asked.

"Sarah carried a lot of pain with her," Steve said. "But she didn't talk about it right away. Until I showed up, she didn't talk at all, from what you said."

"She didn't," I agreed. "So you think someone has to show up that will get his attention?"

"But Helena can't show up," Stephanie protested. "She's in a nursing home full-time. She can't go anywhere."

"And we don't even know the full story of what happened between them," I added. "For all we know, Helena really might have started the fire on purpose. Sarah didn't want to be in her house after her father shot her. Mr. Abbott might feel exactly the same way."

"That's my point," Steve said. "Look, I want to help him out, too, but until we know more of the story, we can't be sure we're going about it the right way. We need to ask anyone we can about him, before we ask him ourselves."

"If Miss Mollie's is open, we could ask her," Stephanie said. Steve and I looked at each other.

"She won't be open long, if she hasn't closed already," I said. "It's summer, so she might stay open until seven. We'll need to eat and run."

Almost on cue, Tina appeared again, this time carrying our plates. "BLT," she said, placing mine in front of me, "and two burgers," she finished, as she put down Steve's and Stephanie's. "Y'all need anything else?" she asked.

I could tell she was busy; the diner wasn't that crowded, but there were also fewer wait staff. "We're fine. Thank you," I replied. She smiled, reflexively, and left us again.

Steve was already starting in on his burger, while Stephanie was salting her fries. I took a bite of my sandwich; it was good, if unremarkable, like most everything Cleve's served.

I was trying to eat quickly without eating quickly – we all were – so that ten minutes later, when Tina came to check on us, we were all nearly finished. "Y'all must've been hungry," she remarked, her eyebrows raised.

"We were," Steve said. "Could we get our check, please?"

Tina smiled, this time genuinely. "With appetites like that, I thought for sure you'd want some dessert," she said.

"Usually we would," Steve said. "But we just realized we have to be somewhere by seven, and it's past six-thirty now."

Tina's expression drooped into mock disappointment, but her eyes still held the smile. "All right, baby. I'll have your check at the counter."

As we got up to go, Steve counted out six dollars for her tip, and left it on the table. Stephanie looked at him in amazement.

"Our whole check isn't but fourteen dollars," she said. "Why did you tip her so much?"

"Because we would have stayed for dessert if we could," he answered. "Besides, she has to work harder tonight, since there's not as many wait staff." He paused. "And this place may not be here in a year or two. Anything I can do to help."

"You're too nice for your own good," I observed, hoping he wouldn't catch my full meaning. Fortunately, he didn't, as Stephanie was distracting him.

Steve paid our bill, and he and Stephanie got in his truck. I followed them in mine out onto Pulaski Street, and drove the three or four blocks south from Cleve's to the shopping center where Mollie's was located. As we parked, we could see that the lights were still on. I looked at my watch, and saw that it was ten minutes to seven.

Steve and Stephanie were already getting out of his truck. I opened my door and hopped out, and the three of us crossed the parking lot and entered the floral shop.

Mollie's son, Ambrose, was clearing up as they were getting ready to close. I guessed that Mollie was, as before, sitting in the back, behind the curtain that was drawn closed behind the register. Ambrose looked up when we entered, giving us a small, polite smile.

"Haven't seen you since you were last around asking questions," he observed in his deep voice. "Did you find out any more about Miss Beckwith?"

"We did," Steve answered. "I think we know almost everything about her now. We're looking into another story from that same time."

Ambrose cocked an eyebrow at us. "Does this story have a name?" he asked.

"Albert Abbott," Stephanie said. "He died in 1957, in a house fire."

Ambrose's smile slowly faded as he studied us, one by one. "This shop opened four years after that," he said slowly. "My mother might know something, but I don't expect it would be more than hearsay. I'll ask her." He paused. "Has anyone left flowers for Mr. Abbott recently?"

Somehow, I knew: Ambrose had some idea of what we were investigating, and he knew full well that Mr. Abbott's grave hadn't had a visitor in a long time. In short, he was telling us that if we wanted answers, we should buy some flowers. Smart business policy, I reflected.

"Stephanie, can you pick out a bouquet for Mr. Abbott?" I asked. "Steve and I can ask Miss Mollie."

She looked as though she was about to protest, then reconsidered. I knew Steve would be the right person to approach Mollie, since his efforts with Sarah had freed her from an awful burden of angry guilt. "All right," she said, as Ambrose ushered us into the shop's back room.

MISS MOLLIE HAD evidently overheard the entire conversation, and she looked us both over, her eyes lingering briefly on Steve. "I'm glad to see you again," she said quietly. "You made my days a little brighter."

"Ours too," Steve answered. "We're hoping we can do that for someone else."

"Well, now," Mollie said, folding her aged hands in her lap, "I'll tell you what I can, though Lord knows that's not much. This shop hadn't opened yet."

"What do you remember?" I asked.

"Albert Abbott served in the Second World War," Mollie said, then looked again at us both. "Most every man of fighting age did, but I expect you know all that. Still, when a war veteran died in those days, it was a big deal in this town. Not like today," she added, a little wistfully.

"Was there any kind of rumor about the fire?" Steve asked. Mollie cut a glance toward him.

"Of course there was," she said. "There were always whispers about Helena and Albert, at least after he died, but never anything that was fact. They didn't grow up here, and Albert didn't graduate school until after the war, after he and Helena were married. A lot of GI's finished school after they came back.

"I remember they were nice enough people. Albert was a mechanic at the garage just north of town, on the Stockville Highway. They never had any children. They went to the First Methodist Church, and lived off Highway 255, in one of the neighborhoods built there after the GIs came back. They were just regular townsfolk, until the night their house burned."

"Do you know what happened after?" I asked.

"There was some question about how the fire started, even before the ashes had cooled," Mollie said slowly. "Some folks gossiped that Helena set the fire, but I never believed it, even though she left town as soon as the funeral was done." She shook a gnarled finger at me. "First Methodist wouldn't allow him to be buried in their cemetery, because of the rumors, so poor Helena had to beg First New Jerusalem to let her bury Albert there. Even then, they put him way across the road, with the Beckwiths and some other people with scurrilous stories." Her chin lifted in defiant reproval. "I'd've left too, if they'd treated me so."

Steve and I looked at each other. "Did you know where she went?" he asked.

"I'd heard she went to live up north, in the mountains," Mollie replied. "After that, I don't know."

"We found where she lives now," I said. "She's in a nursing home in Lavonia – northeast corner of Georgia. We're going to try to see her this weekend."

Mollie studied us some more, her eyelids drooping slightly as though she had grown sleepy, but I knew she was still alert. "If you find out what all really happened, I'd appreciate it if you come back and tell me about it," she said. "I never could really believe Helena Abbott started that fire."

"Yes, ma'am," I replied, and looked at my watch. "Your shop's about to close. We're just going to take a bouquet for Mr. Abbott's grave and go."

"All right, now," she replied, and closing her eyes, she leaned back in her chair. Steve and I came out from the curtain just as Ambrose was wrapping the flowers Stephanie had picked out. It was a simple floral assortment, colorful, but not too terribly expensive. Before Stephanie could reach into her purse, Steve was offering to pay for them.

Ambrose rang up the transaction, and gave us each his small smile. "I don't know exactly why you're looking into all these past histories," he said, "but as long as you keep putting flowers on those graves, it's fine by me."

I smiled back, as did Steve and Stephanie. As we filed out, Ambrose turned the door sign from "Open" to "Closed,", and locked the door behind us.

There were still some thirty minutes to sunset. Steve and I and Stephanie all looked at one another. "There's time to go to the cemetery," I ventured.

"Then let's go," Steve said. Stephanie followed, carrying the bouquet.

As we drove north, first through the square, and then out Highway 255 toward New Jerusalem, I realized that I envied Steve just a little. When we had been hunting down Sarah's story, Stephanie had always accompanied me. Now, the two of them were close – much closer than she and I had ever been – and I was the one riding alone. Even if Joey had joined us, he would have had Lori along; if anything, those two were even closer, and had been since they were both freshmen.

Fortunately, I didn't have time for much of a pity party. We arrived at the cemetery and pulled into the park in just a few minutes. Stephanie had already left the truck and gone around the fence. I looked over at Steve.

"She always was the one that had this place memorized," I commented. He chuckled.

"I remember. The only ones she didn't know about were hidden," he answered. "What gets me is that Mr. Abbott's grave is much more in the open. They hid the Beckwiths really well."

"Maybe it's because Albert wasn't a bootlegger," I replied. "Everyone knew what Mr. Beckwith was. Some people here might even have suspected what he did to Sarah."

"Ambrose's father knew," Steve said, then looked meaningfully at the church. "Not that he would have been real welcome in there."

As we talked, Stephanie had reached the grave, and placed the flowers in the urn set in the memorial stone. She stepped back a few paces from it as Steve climbed over the fence, making his way toward her. I noticed the sun had nearly set. He had almost reached her when the ghosts started materializing; peripherally, I saw several appear in different parts of the cemetery. I was watching Steve and Stephanie, so that when Mr. Abbott arrived, I saw it at once, though I was about a hundred feet away.

Usually, Mr. Abbott would appear out of thin air directly over his grave, dusting the shoulders of his suit jacket – not that there was anything soiling it – and walk straight into the church without engaging anyone, living or dead. He repeated the first part of his routine, and seemed about to turn around, when he saw the flowers in the urn.

For a moment he froze, staring at them inscrutably, his right hand arrested as it brushed his left arm. After several seconds, his hand dropped from his sleeve, but his eyes never left the bouquet. He was facing away from Steve and Stephanie, so that when he slowly turned, he saw me watching him first, and then noticed them standing only a few feet away.

He never spoke, and I couldn't really see his expression – he was a long way off, and facing to the side – but Stephanie's reaction was immediate. I remembered how she emotional she had been on that morning when Tommy asked us to help him find his ball for the last time. I could tell she was crying again, and Steve was holding her while watching Mr. Abbott, but I never heard any of them speak. After a long pause, the ghost turned toward the church and walked toward it without looking back.

I jumped the fence much as Steve had, and came toward them as fast as I could without running. Stephanie was beginning to calm down a little. Steve looked more stunned than anything else.

"What happened?" I asked. Stephanie looked up at me, red-eyed and sniffling.

"He saw the flowers and – and he just looked at me," she answered, gulping. "I've never seen him show any emotion before."

"He looked surprised, and really, he looked touched." Steve added, his voice thicker than usual. "I don't think anyone has visited him specifically since Helena left. Even the kids who could see him were only coming to see ghosts in general. The flowers were something he's never received before." He sighed. "I wonder now if anyone's left anything here since his funeral."

More tears were running down Stephanie's face. "It was gratitude," she whispered. "His face. He was staring at me, and it was gratitude." She swallowed. "There's a lot more to this story. I have to know, now." She looked up at Steve. "I remember how you felt about Sarah. I understand that now."

She took a deep breath, and disengaged from Steve, and for a few minutes we all looked at each other, and at the flowers on the grave. We didn't say anything, but we all knew we were making a silent agreement: we weren't going to stop until we found a way to get Mr. Abbott home.

CHAPTER THREE

THAT SUNDAY MORNING, I picked up Stephanie and drove to the library, pulling into the parking lot a few minutes before eight. Miss Roberts had already arrived. I parked my truck and we hopped out as she rolled down her window.

"We aren't late, are we?" I asked, even though I knew we weren't. Miss Roberts smiled at us – a rarity – and shook her head.

"No, I just got here early," she replied. "I don't go places very often, and I must say I've been looking forward to this."

"So are we," I answered. I glanced toward Stephanie. "Front or back?"

"Back," she replied. "You're a lot taller than I am."

I nodded, though it wasn't really a concern. Miss Roberts drove a huge four-door sedan that dated to the mid-1970s. It was immaculately clean, and clearly well-maintained, but something occurred to me as we got in.

"We can chip in for gas," I said. I knew her car probably got horrible mileage. She gave me another smile.

"I'd appreciate that," she replied. "Librarians don't make the big money, like janitors."

I laughed, not only at the joke, but because I had never heard her make one before. Stephanie was chuckling as well.

Miss Roberts maneuvered her land yacht out onto Highway 255 and headed north.

"It might be a little faster taking the Interstate to Tuckerton," she observed as she drove, "but this is a prettier drive, and we'll have enough highway once we get going toward Lavonia."

I had to agree, in more ways than one. I knew Steve usually took the back roads to get to McDowell Mills, in no small part because the Interstates – I-285 and I-75 – both featured heavy traffic and a lot of drivers who thought the speed limit was a minimum. He was able to drive on them, but he hated it.

We reached New Jerusalem First Methodist, and were stopped by the traffic light. As we waited, I pointed toward the back of the cemetery on our left. "We found Sarah's grave over there, at the hedge," I told Miss Roberts.

She looked over at me, smiling, but sadly. "I haven't visited it yet, but I will, after we get back."

"It's not easy to get into her family plot," Stephanie said from the back. "We never even knew it was there, until Steve found it. The hedge grew up around it, and the church never cleared it away."

The light changed, and Miss Roberts accelerated north again. "Honestly, that doesn't surprise me much," she said softly. We all became quiet, looking out at the fields and trees as we continued on our way. After some minutes, the terrain began to change, becoming almost mountainous. Miss Roberts's face, which had been pensive, became more animated again.

"This is one of the most unusual geologic areas in Georgia," she commented. "The upwelling that formed Stone Mountain actually created a line of hills that run through DeKalb County, though the others aren't nearly as large."

"I'm familiar with Stone Mountain," Stephanie said. "The guys in Kelleyville like to go up there."

Miss Roberts snorted again. "That certainly doesn't surprise me," she answered. "Stone Mountain doesn't exactly have the best history. It's a shame, because it's unlike anywhere else in the country. There are a few more mountains that run south from it – Panola Mountain and Arabia Mountain are both state parks – and there's also a big quarry that probably would be a park if it hadn't been ruined by all the stonecutting there."

"I never knew about that one," I said. I knew about the other two parks; when I was a kid, my parents sometimes went to Arabia Mountain for picnics, though they hadn't gone since I entered middle school.

"The whole southern part of the county looks like it's in the Appalachians – a lot of valleys and hills. It's different from anyplace else around Atlanta." Miss Roberts lapsed into silence again as we drove through the wooded hills, looking at the warm, sunlit foliage and shaded streams running through the occasional wide, stony ravines. I hadn't been through there often, and it was a lot prettier looking than the pastures and farmland that comprised most of McDowell Mills.

All at once, we emerged from what somehow felt like an almost prehistoric landscape, and were back in suburbia – strip malls, chain restaurants, and a lot more traffic seemed to materialize from nowhere as we approached Interstate 20. It was something of a disappointment, and before I could say so, Stephanie beat me to it, murmuring, "Back in civilization."

Miss Roberts smiled. "I know exactly what you mean," she said, still watching the road as we continued north. In fifteen more minutes, we reached Tuckerton, and were driving up Main Street toward the local high school. We could easily see Steve's refurbished truck in the empty parking lot, with him standing beside it, and Miss Roberts was able to pilot her huge vehicle straight into the lot behind him as he waved to us. He was carrying what looked like a half-dozen boxes of tissues with him.

He hopped into the rear seat behind Miss Roberts, saying "Hi!" as he stacked the tissue boxes in the floorboard, before Stephanie hugged him. I glanced toward Miss Roberts, who was watching them in the mirror.

"You two better behave back there," she said, as she pulled back out of the parking lot and continued north on the four-lane road that would take us to I-85.

"Yes, ma'am," Steve answered, but he was smiling, and after the initial hug, they only held hands as we drove. "I brought the tissues for the folks at the nursing home," he said to Miss Roberts, who nodded her approval.

"It's two hours from here to Lavonia, and it's not very scenic," she commented as the entrance to the interstate hove into view a few minutes later. "Hopefully the farms near the highway don't smell as bad as I remember they did twenty years ago."

"Ugh. I hope you're right," I replied, and we lapsed into silence.

THE TRIP UP to Lavonia was uneventful, and there was little conversation on the way. Once out of the suburbs surrounding Atlanta, the countryside emptied out, with farmland alternating with pine woods and the occasional bottomland. I could tell we were gaining altitude steadily as we drove northeast, and to our left, we could dimly make out the southern end of the Great Smoky Mountains, as hazy as their name implied.

Some ninety minutes later, just before the border with South Carolina, Miss Roberts steered off the highway onto the Lavonia exit. It ended in an overpass, with a rail track running in front of us alongside Georgia Highway 17. She turned right, toward the town, as the highway narrowed into one of the two main streets that paralleled the tracks in the town's center, about a mile off of the interstate. At West Avenue, Miss Roberts turned left, crossing the tracks just south of the unused rail station, and then turned right. Two blocks ahead, the street curved to the left and became Hartwell Road, and just past the curve, we could see what looked like a small, weathered, butter-colored brick house with an arched loft. The arch featured the words "CARNEGIE LIBRARY" in relief.

Miss Roberts maneuvered her car into the nearly-empty parking lot and looked around. "I'm supposed to meet the librarian here." She glanced at her watch. "We're a few minutes early, so you can go on ahead. You know where you're supposed to go?"

"Yes, ma'am," Stephanie answered. "The nursing home's on Parkertown Road, less than half a mile from here. We can walk."

"Yeah," Steve added. "I need to walk a bit anyway." He looked toward Miss Roberts' reflection in the rear-view mirror. "How long do you think you'll be touring the Library? I'd hate to leave you sitting here waiting on us."

"Oh, I think it will be a while," Miss Roberts said. "You kids go on now."

We got out of the car and looked briefly over the library grounds, then at each other as we started down Hartwell Road, away from town. We each carried two tissue boxes. I knew what we were all thinking, and I finally had to say it: "It's a good thing she came up here when she did. That library isn't in very good shape."

"I know! I don't understand why the town doesn't do more to take care of it," Stephanie said. "It's a piece of real history. Not a lot of places have something like that."

"Lavonia might be a lot more like McDowell Mills than we expected," Steve said. "But really, to me, it looks more like Jackson Creek. It's poorer than where you guys live, and it's not changing. The whole town's probably looked the same since World War II." He paused. "And that building looks like it has worse problems than just the paint and woodwork. There were puddles next to the walls. If it has a basement, I'd bet they have leakage in there."

Parkertown Road turned out to be only two blocks away from the library. We turned left, crossing the almost empty street, and found ourselves on a shaded, residential avenue that looked like a baby-boom-era neighborhood – comfortable, staid, and very, very dated. We all looked around ourselves as we walked.

"I feel like I just stepped out of a time machine," Stephanie said in a low voice.

"In a way, we did," Steve observed. "McDowell Mills has at least reached the Seventies, and is trying to get to the Eighties. Tuckerton's in the Nineties. But this place? Late Forties or early Fifties."

I didn't say anything. They had both described the place exactly as I would have. It wasn't unpleasant, but one look at the neighborhood told me a lot about the residents – mostly older, longtime citizens, with their own way of doing pretty much everything.

"This is like the North Georgia equivalent of the area around New Jerusalem," Steve added. He wasn't wrong.

We lapsed into silence as we walked the quarter of a mile between Hartwell Road and the converted elementary school that housed the New Star Assisted Living facility. Steve snorted at the name – "New Star? More like Nighty-Night" – which earned him a swat from Stephanie as we approached the double front doors. The building itself was tiny, maybe half the size of the cookie-cutter elementary school Stephanie and I had attended, and was clearly of the same vintage as the surrounding neighborhoods.

We went inside, and the first thing that hit us was the smell. If you've ever been in a nursing home, or a long-term ward in a hospital, you'll know what that smell is. This facility at least did its level best to counter it, but instead of eliminating the odor, the staff evidently had deployed copious amounts of competing fragrances in the hope of drowning it out. Those efforts were at best a conditional success. We looked at each other for a moment – Stephanie with evident dismay, Steve with resignation – before I shrugged and led the others toward the receptionist's desk.

The woman seated there was not what I would have expected. She was no more than thirty, and bore a physical similarity to Stephanie, though older. She wore a brightly-colored blouse and jacket with a long skirt, had a mass of blonde hair with pink highlights, and glasses that might have belonged to someone in the neighborhood outside around the time they moved in. A placard in front of her desk displayed her name: Chloe Martin. I had to smile at her; her presence, and demeanor, brightened the place considerably. She smiled back, and looked at each of us in turn. "Are you here visiting someone in particular?" she asked.

"Yes," I answered. I glanced toward Steve, then continued. "We were hoping to talk with one of your residents, Ms. Helena Abbott."

"Are you friends of the family?" she asked, still friendly, but very slightly watchful.

"Not exactly," Stephanie said. "We're from the McDowell Mills High School Historical Society. We've been researching our local cemeteries and putting together a history of as many people from the town as we can find."

"Ms. Abbott lived there a long time ago," Steve added. "Her husband passed away there, about thirty-five years ago now, and she moved here not long after that. We were hoping she could tell us more about him. We know he was born in Jackson Creek, and he served in the Army Air Corps during the war."

Chloe's smile had faded noticeably, but she didn't seem unfriendly. Rising to her feet, she called into the office behind her, "Gladys, can you watch the front for me for a minute?" Without waiting for a response, she came out from the desk, saying "this way. I'll ask whether she'd like to talk with you."

She led us down one of the old school hallways, which were decorated with multiple bulletin boards and plenty of reproduction paintings. I wasn't sure whether these were intended to brighten the place, or counter the acoustics common to most schools built at that time, but they were effective either way. Instead of feeling institutional, the place had an odd but welcoming feeling to it. I realized that I was no longer noticing the smell as much as before.

We turned right, moving past what had apparently been the library. It had been converted into a common area, with bookshelves and board games lining the walls. I glimpsed two tables full of card players, all of them at least in their seventies, but surprisingly animated for that. Continuing past them, we turned left, passing several doors on each side until we reached Room 116 on the right-hand side of the hall. Below the room number, two placards read, "B. Harrison" and "H. Abbott."

Chloe tapped on the door, and stuck her head inside, and said, "Hi, Janie. There's some students here from a school in McDowell Mills, who wanted to know if they could interview your Aunt Helena."

There wasn't a spoken response, but Chloe stepped back from the door as a dark-haired, blue-eyed girl about our own age brushed past her and stared at us.

"Who are you?" she asked, not indicating any one of us in particular. She didn't seem very friendly.

"Hi," Stephanie said, slightly hesitantly. "My name's Stephanie Johnson, and this is Steve Smith –" she motioned toward Steve – "and Chad Campbell. We're students at McDowell Mills High School, and members of the school's Historical Society."

"Janie Sawyer. Why do you want to talk with my aunt?" Janie asked suspiciously.

Steve and I exchanged a glance. Stephanie answered, "we've been researching the history of McDowell Mills – not just the big events, or the important people. We're trying to learn about everyone we can, to get a narrative of what everyday life was really like for the people who lived there." She took a deep breath. "Your aunt's husband, Albert, served in the Army Air Corps, and grew up in Jackson Creek. He died in a house fire, and your aunt moved here after that. We just wanted to know if she could tell us more about him, and what life was like in the McDowell Mills that they lived in."

Janie still looked suspicious, and glared at each of us in turn, before her stare settled on me. I wasn't comfortable at all, but I returned her look as expressionlessly as I could – which wasn't easy. In spite of her obvious mistrust, I couldn't help noticing how pretty she was.

She stared at me for several seconds before addressing Stephanie, this time in a low voice. "My aunt said the people in McDowell Mills were awful. She said that when she moved away, the people living there were whispering that she had set the fire so that she could kill her husband and collect the insurance money."

"We don't believe that," Steve said, before she could say more. "We know exactly what the people in McDowell Mills are like. We don't like the town any more than she did – that's one of the main reasons we started the Historical Society, so that we could get to the truth of a lot of stories like that."

Her expression softened very slightly, and she seemed about to answer, when a voice floated out of the room behind her: "oh, let them in, Janie girl. I don't mind talking with them."

Janie's eyebrows raised, and she replied, "all right, Aunt Helena," over her shoulder. She was still looking at me, and she whispered, "please, don't upset her."

"We'll do our best. If something we ask makes her uncomfortable, we'll change the subject," I said quickly. She smiled humorlessly at me, then nodded, and led us into the room.

Helena's room was a converted classroom, divided into two semi-private alcoves with a small, shared lavatory closet installed where the teacher's supply cabinet had probably been. It was obviously not an optimal design, but functional given the space the nursing home had to work with. I guessed that price had played a large factor in the building's conversion.

Helena herself was sitting up in bed, wearing a flowered, cotton dressing gown with her thin, gray hair pinned up and glasses not dissimilar to Chloe's. We knew that she was getting close to eighty, but still retained the vestiges of long-ago prettiness, and she had a frailty to her that indicated that she probably wouldn't be around much longer. Still, her eyes were clear and sharp as she looked each of us over in turn.

"I won't be needing those," she said, motioning toward the tissue boxes, "but it's thoughtful of you to bring them. Quite a few folks here don't have anyone to bring them the things they need."

"We knew that might be the case," Steve answered her. "We thought that if you didn't need them, someone here would, so we brought enough for several."

"Well, you were right." Helena nodded. "I heard you saying that you were from McDowell Mills, and you wanted to know about my husband Albert."

"Well, yes, ma'am. We knew about his military service, and we also found his gravestone, in the New Jerusalem cemetery. The obituary said he had a wife, and a brother and sister," I replied quietly.

"We tried to find his brother, but he left Jackson Creek in the sixties," Stephanie said. Steve looked askance at her. "You didn't mention that."

"I thought I did. Anyway, no one there has heard from him in ages, and he could be anywhere. We don't even know if he's still living," Stephanie said

"He's not," Helena put in, quietly. "He got TB, and went out west to Arizona – I guess it was 1968 or 1969. He lasted another two years out there before it killed him – they caught it too late, and the medicines didn't do enough to stop it."

"I'm sorry," Steve said. Helena waved her hand negligently.

"That was a long time ago, and honestly, I never much liked him," she said. "He never seemed to have much good to say about anything."

"If you don't mind my asking, how did you meet your husband?" I asked. I could hear Stephanie holding her breath. Helena smiled.

"Albert and I were high-school sweethearts," she said, "and really, grade-school sweethearts as well. I liked him almost from my first day at school. He was very polite, very friendly. Most everyone liked him." She glanced toward Janie. "I was a half-year older than he was, but that never seemed to matter, even when we were children. We just fit together, from the beginning, and it seemed like everyone understood. Usually kids will tease each other, when there's a crush involved, but I guess with Albert and me, everyone decided we just belonged together."

"So you grew up in Jackson Creek," Stephanie said.

"That's right," Helena replied. "We were in school together until Albert turned sixteen, right after tenth grade. He had to drop out after that. The Depression had gotten bad, and Jackson Creek was withering away. It never did fully recover," she said. "When I moved up here, that town was barely half the size it was when we grew up. I had happy memories there, but after the Depression, it was too sad and run down for me to want to visit it anymore."

"It's still like that," Steve said. Helena looked at him oddly for a moment.

"Your accent's different," she said. "Is your family from McDowell Mills?"

"No, ma'am," he replied. "I grew up in Tuckerton, and my family just moved back there. We spent a year in McDowell

Mills, after my uncle died, and we inherited his farm. We had to fix it up enough to be able to sell it."

Helena was studying him carefully, and her eyes widened slightly. "You look like someone I met once or twice, before Albert passed. What was your uncle's name?" she asked.

Steve looked uncertainly at me. "Fred Smith," he answered.

"The same Fred Smith that was working with Bill Beckwith?" she asked. Steve nodded, and a knowing look crossed her lined face.

"Fred Smith was involved in a scandal of his own," Helena observed. "More than one, from what I heard later. When the state police arrested all those people in the sixties, Fred Smith got away clean as a whistle, even though he was neck-deep in cahoots with that Beckwith fellow." She paused. "And that's saying nothing about what happened with Beckwith's daughter."

"We know the full story about her," Steve said. "That was what inspired us to start the Historical Society. Uncle Fred was going to marry her, and bought a farm outside of town for them, but old man Beckwith was planning on using it for whatever he was up to, and they had an argument. Beckwith had a gun, and Sarah got in the way, and he shot her by accident.

"Fred spent years working with Beckwith, getting everything he could on him. He was the one who called in the state police. It made him mean and bitter till the day he died."

Helena's expression had changed. Her eyes were round, and her mouth hung slightly open. She looked to each of us in turn, including Janie, whose suspicious demeanor had softened noticeably.

"Upon my life, I would never have guessed that," she said. "I remember when the Beckwith girl died. Her father had the worst time trying to get any of the local churches to give up a burial plot for his family. He finally had to go to New Jerusalem, and they put her way out away from the church." Her jaw hardened. "Then they did the same thing to me, when I had to lay Albert to rest. They didn't blame me for the fire, not out loud, but I knew what they said amongst themselves." She laughed bitterly. "The insurance barely covered what we owed on the house. I moved up here because I had to. Janie's grandmother – Albert's sister – she understood, and invited me to come live with her. I certainly wasn't going to stay one minute more than I had to in that town."

"Neither did my family," Steve said quietly. "I don't blame you one bit."

"We've visited Albert's marker at New Jerusalem cemetery," Stephanie said. "Enough people have passed away that his grave isn't out by itself anymore." She paused. "They let a hedge grow up around the Beckwiths' plot. We didn't even know it was there until Steve found it. Even now, they don't tend it."

Helena nodded. "As I would expect. That church formed when one awful group of Methodists got into a tiff with another awful group of Methodists." She looked at us each, and then to Janie, before she asked, "what would you like to know about Albert?

"Anything you're willing to tell us," I said, smiling slightly at her. She smiled back.

"Pull up some chairs, then. This might take a little while," she said.

HELENA TALKED WITH us for nearly two hours, telling us about how Albert worked as a mechanic, then joined the Army Air Corps when he turned 18, intending to learn how to repair airplanes. They had drifted apart during that time, as he was stationed first at Mabry Army Airfield in Tallahassee, then at Robins Field south of Macon. When the war started, he remained stateside, training airplane mechanics before they shipped out to the European theater.

Albert left the service in 1945, only a few months before the atomic bomb was dropped on Japan, and returning home, had found that Helena was still in Jackson Creek. They married shortly after. As she was relating that part of the story, I noticed that she had become slightly hesitant, and while I wanted to ask her why, something told me to let her continue. I felt that she could always tell us later.

In 1946, Helena and Albert moved from Jackson Creek to McDowell Mills, which was recovering from the Depression and war more robustly, and Albert went to work as a mechanic in the local garage. At times, he would drive out to the airstrip north of Kelleyville to do some airplane repairs. Between those two jobs, he was able to provide them with a comfortable enough life.

They bought their house in 1954, after Albert had saved enough for them to afford the down payment. It had been on a street off of Highway 255, almost within sight of the library.

She had loved that house, and had hoped to start a family there, but it was not to be – they never had any children. Her face became so sad, as she told us this, that I couldn't help reaching over and taking her hand for a moment. She merely patted my hand, and smiled, and continued with her story.

We were running out of time when we got to 1957, and I knew she might be reluctant to broach the subject of the fire, so I gently interrupted her at that point. "Ms. Abbott, thank you so much for telling us about your husband. Would it be all right if we come back next week?"

She smiled at us again, gratefully surprised. I glanced toward Janie. Her suspicion had melted away, and she was smiling at me, too.

"You be sure to come back," Helena said. "Janie, help me get this pillow moved. I think I'll want a nap before supper."

Janie moved to help her aunt as we stood up, and made our way to the door. Just before we left, I said, "We'll have to check with our families and make sure it's all right for us to come up. If we can't come back next weekend, would another time be all right?"

Helena waved her hand in assent. Janie looked back at me, and I saw her mouth the word, "wait." I nodded, and the three of us filed out. I signaled for Stephanie and Steve to stay where they were, and a few seconds later, Janie came out of the room.

"That was really, really sweet of you," she told us, looking at me. "I was afraid she wouldn't want to talk about it, especially given where you come from. She said it was awful."

"She was exactly right," Steve said. "It's finally beginning to change a little, but that's only because Atlanta has gotten so big that the suburbs go that far out now. The old families are just as rotten as they always were."

"And so are the cops," Stephanie added. Janie laughed.

"Be sure to ask Aunt Helena about the one time Albert got arrested," she said, grinning. "She'll give you an earful."

"All right," I said. The others turned to leave, but she was still watching me, and she said in a much lower voice, "can I have your phone number?"

I admit, I was really startled. She knew how far away I lived, and honestly, I felt a little intimidated by her. She was prettier than any girl I would have tried to date, for one thing. But I remembered that in McDowell Mills, the society was more regimented, and everyone had known each other since kindergarten, so everyone knew their place. Whatever the social structure was in Lavonia, I was outside it. Maybe that was what she saw in me.

"Sure," I answered her. She went quickly back into her aunt's room, returning with a note pad and a pen. I wrote down my name and my full number, handing it to her, before she wrote down her name and number well below mine, and tore off the bottom half of the sheet.

"It was nice to meet you," she said. "Hope you can make it here next week."

"Oh, we will," I replied. She gave me one last smile, and then returned to her aunt's room. I turned to leave, and was met with two huge grins from Steve and Stephanie as we made our way back to the front of the facility.

"I wouldn't have thought *that* was going to happen, when we first got here," Stephanie said. I had to admit, I wouldn't have, either.

CHAPTER FOUR

I HADN'T PLANNED on calling Steve or Stephanie before Tuesday, but I realized I didn't want to wait that long to call Janie. I couldn't just phone her out of the blue – I didn't know her that well, and I thought I should have some reason to call her. That meant that we would have to plan our next trip to Lavonia as quickly as we could.

With that in mind, I called Steve late Monday afternoon, hoping he wouldn't be at work. Thankfully, he was at home tinkering with his truck again, and his mom called him to the phone. "Hey, Chad. You call that girl yet?"

"I *knew* you were going to ask that," I replied. "Not yet. I thought we should have something planned, so that I don't just call her and not have anything to say."

"Makes sense," Steve said. "It looks like you made a good first impression with her."

"I think so," I answered. "But it might just be that I'm not from Lavonia. Being new didn't hurt you any when you met Stephanie, did it?"

"That's true. And you know a little bit about her aunt, the same way Stephanie knew a bit about Uncle Fred," he added. "I'd be curious to hear what she knows about the Toccoa Falls flood. We never even got to ask about that. Janie was too young to remember it, but she would have grown up hearing about it."

"Yeah. And you know how kids are with ghost stories. I remember you thought we were kidding you about the ghosts at New Jerusalem." I thought for a moment. "If Janie's seen anything like that, it would be worth learning about it."

"Maybe," Steve said. "And I think Lavonia's probably got some skeletons in its closet, but I didn't get the same feeling about the place that I did about New Jerusalem. It's weird, and I don't know exactly how to describe it."

I was puzzled by this. "How do you mean?" I asked.

I heard him sigh as he considered. "It feels – older, I guess," he finally replied. "The land up there is less developed than around Atlanta. The mountains are closer, and the towns don't sprawl into each other. I think it might be really scary to be out in the woods alone up there."

I hadn't really thought much about that, but as he said it, I realized that he was right – there was something about the whole area that seemed to remember before any European feet had ever walked there. It didn't feel evil or malevolent, but it did feel distant.

Steve spoke again. "I went to a cemetery about ten years ago, down in Savannah, that was *really* old. One of my mother's relatives was being buried there. I remember looking around at some of the gravestones. There were people there who died before the people buried at New Jerusalem were even born. That place felt like Lavonia feels to me. It's almost like something there is just waiting for the people to go away, so that it can…" his voice trailed off.

"Can what?" I asked.

He was silent for maybe ten seconds before he said, "so it can be quiet again, I think." His voice was low. "That was how the cemetery felt – as if it wouldn't make me leave, but it just wanted everyone to go away, so that it would be quiet."

"I never felt anything like that here," I said. "I kind of understand what you're saying, though."

"I don't know that we're going to find any ghosts in Lavonia," Steve said. "I'm not sure what we'll find there, but it scares me a bit."

"I can't see that it would be any scarier than seeing real ghosts," I pointed out. He chuckled.

"You might be right," he said. "But we need to work out how we're going back. We promised we would be there this weekend, so we have to get there. I already checked with my mom and dad, and they're OK with me taking the truck, but I only have two seatbelts."

I thought about that. "You want to meet tomorrow at the library? We're all going to need to figure this trip out. I know for sure I'm going, even if I have to go by myself."

"Why am I not surprised?" Steve said sardonically, and then laughed. "I can't make tomorrow, though. I can get there for lunch Wednesday."

"OK. I'll run that by Stephanie." I paused. "Do you think we should tell Mr. Abbott about Helena?"

Steve paused again. "Not yet," he answered at last. "Helena didn't tell us anything about what happened to him. And I think something else is going on there, too. She kind of skipped over the time while he was in the service, for one thing."

"I noticed that, too," I said. "Wednesday noon, then?"

"Sure," he replied. "But let's meet somewhere besides Cleve's this time, OK?"

I considered that. "There's a buffet place that just opened in Stockville," I finally said. "It's not much farther from New Jerusalem than Cleve's, and we haven't been there before."

"All right. You going to bring Stephanie, or should I pick her up?" he asked.

I thought about that, but only for a second. "I'll get her," I answered. There was silence for a moment.

"OK. Wednesday noon. But I think you should call that girl before Thursday. Unless you're not interested," he added. I could tell he knew very well that wasn't the case.

"Once we know the plan, I'll tell her," I said. "See you Wednesday."

I CALLED STEPHANIE and made our plans to meet Steve in Stockville, then stared for a few seconds at the phone after she hung up. I knew I was stalling, worried that Janie might have reconsidered about me, but I also knew that there wasn't anything I could do about it if she had. We were still going to talk with Helena again, Janie or no Janie.

I took out my wallet and fished out the folded half sheet of note paper with her number on it. Hoping I wasn't making a horrible mistake, I punched in the number. It took the call several seconds to connect – it was long-distance – and I almost hung up before the second ring, but the line clicked on before I could chicken out. "Hello?" asked a voice much older than Janie's. I realized that I was speaking to Mr. Abbott's sister.

"Hello, Ms. Sawyer. My name is Chad Campbell, and I'm calling to speak to Janie, please," I heard myself say. I was surprised to hear a chuckle in her reply.

"Yes, Janie told me about you. She's been waiting for you to call," she answered. In the background, I could hear Janie's voice. "Oh, all right, here," she said, not to me.

"Hello, Chad," she said. For a moment I almost forgot to speak.

"Hi, Janie," I finally managed. I hoped my voice didn't sound like a croak, but I realized how nervous I was. I took a deep breath to steady myself. "Steve and Stephanie are working out when we can get up there on Saturday. We were going to try to be there by about ten."

"That'd be OK," she replied. "Do you want to meet at New Star, or someplace else?"

"New Star's OK, as long as your aunt doesn't mind morning visitors," I said. "We don't want to impose on her."

"I'll tell her tomorrow." She paused for a moment. "She was so happy to have you come visit. Most of her friends have already died, so usually, the only visitors she gets are me and my grandmother."

I thought about that for a second. "Your parents don't come see her?" I asked.

There was a long silence. I realized I'd asked the wrong question, and was about to try to backtrack when she sighed. "I'll tell you about that when you come up."

"OK," I answered, then added, "look, I'm sorry if I said something wrong. I really didn't mean to upset you."

"It's all right," she said. "I would have had to tell you about it anyway. After you visit Aunt Helena, we can go have lunch and I'll fill you in." She paused. "It's kind of personal, so if it's OK for just the two of us…" her voice trailed off.

"I think it'll be fine," I said, thankful that I could reassure her. "Steve and Stephanie have been dating since the spring, so I think they'll be glad to get some alone time."

"Good," she replied, and I could hear the relief in her voice. "It's not that I don't like them or anything, it's just that this is something I don't talk about much."

"I think I understand," I said, wondering how she'd react if she knew the truth of our association with the Abbotts. "We can talk then."

"All right," she said, then added with a rush, "I'm really looking forward to seeing you."

"I know I understand that," I said, laughing slightly. "I feel the same way."

"Saturday morning, then. Bye," she said, and hung up before I could answer.

THE FOLLOWING EVENING, I picked up Stephanie at home and drove ten miles to Stockville. It was a town in the same county as McDowell Mills, but was closer to Atlanta, and had outgrown the county seat as the suburbs had moved slowly outward. Additionally, Stockville had never had the kind of social structure in place that would stifle growth and change – a condition that the liquor store right past the city-limits sign made clear.

"That's probably the most popular store in McDowell Mills," Stephanie said. I chuckled.

"Nah," I replied. "They go to the one up near Ellenton, to make sure no one sees them."

Stephanie laughed. Skewering our local town's moral façade had always been a source of amusement for us, and for most of our friends as well. It wasn't as though any of us planned to stay there, once we were finished with school. "New Jerusalem probably has someone parked across the street copying down license plate numbers," Stephanie said.

"Wouldn't surprise me," I responded. The restaurant – Bryan's Steaks and Buffet – was only a little way past the liquor store, and within a minute, we had parked. Steve was waiting outside the front doors, and of course Stephanie ran to meet him. At least she had learned to slow up before she reached him, as she nearly knocked him down the first couple of times they had been together after he had moved back to Tuckerton. She gave him a kiss, but not a long one, before we all went inside.

We had gotten a table and filled our plates before Steve asked, "so. You talked to Janie?"

"Yeah," I answered. "She said Helena was really happy we came to visit her, and wants us to come back."

"That's good. I was worried she might not want to tell us more than she did," Stephanie said. "How about Janie? Did you talk with her, too?"

"Yeah," I replied. She looked at me carefully.

"You don't seem that excited," she remarked. "She really acted as though she liked you. And she was really pretty, too."

I wasn't sure yet whether I wanted to say anything more about her, but I knew I had to say something or else Stephanie would never let it go, and we really needed to plan our trip. "She said Helena would be willing to talk with us in the morning, around ten," I said. "After that, she wanted us to go to lunch – we can all go together, but she wanted us to take separate tables, so that she can talk with just me."

Stephanie's eyes lit up, and she looked up at Steve, who was grinning. "Wow. That sounds promising."

"It is," I hedged. "At least, I hope it is."

He gave me a funny look that Stephanie missed, before the three of us went into the restaurant.

THE REST OF THE week passed uneventfully. One last call each to Steve and Stephanie on Friday finalized our plans, and when I called Janie to confirm everything with her, she seemed happier to speak with me, though still somewhat guarded. I honestly didn't know what to make of it, and when I went early Saturday morning to pick Stephanie up, I still didn't know what I expected.

Steve, however, obviously had something on his mind, and when we reached his home in Tuckerton an hour later, he had barely buckled his seatbelt before he asked, "How's Janie?"

Stephanie looked up at me expectantly, and I glanced briefly at them as I wheeled the truck onto Norcross Road toward the Interstate. "She's fine," I answered. "Something's up, and I don't know what, but I don't think it has anything to do with me. At least not directly."

"I was thinking about that," Steve said. "I went to the library in Tuckerton yesterday to research the flood. It was in 1977, and it killed thirty-nine people." He paused. "She would have been a baby then. I kind of wonder if she had family that died in the flood. You said Mr. Abbott's obituary mentioned that he had a nephew."

I thought about that. "She didn't say anything about any of that," I said. "I suppose she'll tell us more when we go to lunch."

"I'm really looking forward to this," Stephanie said. Her tone matched her thought, but I don't think she realized that Steve was apprehensive about it. I asked him, "What's eating you? You seem a bit out of sorts."

Steve sighed, and Stephanie looked at him with sudden, slight worry. "Steve, are you all right?"

"I'm fine," he answered. "It's just that when I was looking up the stories about the dam break, it creeped me out a little – especially with the vibe in that place. I'd think it was nothing, except…"

"Except what?" Stephanie asked. Steve looked sidelong at her. I glanced at them both as I turned onto Interstate 85.

"The whole reason we're going to Lavonia is because of a ghost," Steve said. "A lot of people don't even believe they exist, because they've never seen one. We have." He paused for a minute. "I just wonder how much else is out there that we don't see, or haven't seen yet. Lavonia almost seems haunted to me, and not like New Jerusalem."

"I didn't really feel that," Stephanie said. "It felt like time had passed it by, sure, but I didn't feel anything else. The place was…" her voice trailed away, before she finished her own sentence: "Quaint. The neighborhood where New Star is. It's quaint."

Steve laughed a little at that. "That's actually not a bad word for it. And you're right, it wasn't that neighborhood that was messing with me. It's what's outside of town, especially up closer to the mountains, that's making me wonder."

"Where was this dam break, exactly?" I asked. "Was it in the town?"

"It was north of where we're going," he answered. "Toccoa Falls is about 20 miles north of Lavonia, just past Toccoa, right where the mountains start. The dam was just off campus. It broke in the middle of the night, after a load of rain had fallen, so no one knew it was coming." He paused. "It looked almost like tornado damage. Scary."

"Did they fix the dam?" Stephanie asked.

"The dam was built to make a reservoir," Steve answered. "After the dam failed, the reservoir was drained and the dam was removed, so it won't ever happen again."

"Good," Stephanie said, fervently. I glanced at her. Evidently she found my half-smile objectionable.

"Don't start," she warned me. "A lot of people died in that flood. I wouldn't want to be somewhere that that could happen again."

"The dam broke after something like seven inches of rain fell in less than a week," Steve objected. "It was all the runoff from the higher elevations that filled the reservoir up, and from what I read, the dam was in lousy shape, wasn't being kept up, and people weren't as safety-conscious then. It took stuff like that happening before safety really started being taken seriously."

Stephanie fell silent, looking back and forth between us. I hoped I hadn't ruined the trip for them, because I was beginning to feel nervous, knowing that I'd be seeing Janie again soon.

THE TRIP WAS LESS interesting than when Miss Roberts drove, but it still seemed to fly by, and less than an hour and a half later, I was steering along the same exit ramp we had taken before. Lavonia was the same as before, but I felt a very slight chill as we steered onto Hartwell Road. I glanced toward Steve, who looked back, and said, "I think I understand what you meant."

"Don't miss the turn!" Stephanie said sharply, and I signaled – a bit late, but there was no one on the road to notice – and turned onto Parkertown Road again. The anachronistic, postwar-era feel to the neighborhood hadn't changed.

"This place probably felt dated when it was built," Steve observed. No one replied, and within seconds, I was parking the truck in New Star's old faculty parking lot, now barely half-full.

We got out, and made our way to the door. For some reason, I had expected Janie to be with Helena in her room, and I was pleasantly surprised to see her waiting at Chloe's desk. Even better, she was wearing a flowered sundress that might have been laughed at in McDowell Mills, but fit perfectly with the atmosphere of Lavonia. I smiled at her, and she gave me a glowing smile in return.

Out of the corner of my eye, I saw Stephanie nudge Steve with her elbow, so I decided to speak first. "Hi, Janie. You told your aunt Helena that we're coming, right?"

She snorted, somehow making the noise cute. "No, of course not. I thought we'd surprise her." Her smile turned slightly mischievous, then softened. "I told her two days ago. She's been looking forward to it ever since." She glanced down at her dress, slightly abashed. "And she told me she'd give me what for if I didn't dress nice to see you."

"Remind me to thank her for that," I heard myself say. This time it was Steve who snorted, and an awkward, momentary silence fell, until Janie took my arm and said, "come on, she's really excited."

I let her steer me toward Helena's room, still a bit bemused. I could hear Stephanie whispering something to Steve, but the blood pounding in my ears was too loud for me to catch what she said. I wasn't expecting what I saw when we entered: Janie, or someone at New Star, had fixed her hair and makeup, and dressed her in a bright, flowered robe. She sat on the side of her bed with a pleased, almost expectant smile on her face. There were three chairs beside the wall facing her – someone had borrowed them from the commons – and she motioned us toward them as Janie sat down beside her. She looked nothing like her aunt – I supposed that they weren't blood relatives – but it was clear that years before, Helena had been at least as pretty as her niece.

We all sat facing her, glancing back and forth at each other, until Helena said quietly, "Your visit last week was the first time in years that someone's come to see me."

"We're just glad you were willing to talk to us," Stephanie answered. "It might have been easier for you to send us away, given where we came from."

"Well, that was a long time ago," she said, and looked toward me, studying me for a few moments. "And Janie here spends so much time taking care of her two old ladies when she's not in school. She doesn't have a lot of time for friends, and you three seem like nice, smart types."

Janie looked slightly embarrassed, until Steve nodded. "When my uncle died, my family took over his farm, and when we first moved there, I felt totally alone. I was lucky that Chad and Stephanie –" he motioned toward us – "and their friends, they kind of took me in. I didn't have a car when I lived in Tuckerton, so until I could fix my uncle's truck, I had to ride the bus to school. It was bad."

Janie smiled at him. "I know what that's like," she said. She didn't say more, and after a moment, Helena looked at me again. "So. What more would you like to know?"

"Well…" I glanced toward Janie apprehensively, but she just smiled again and nodded to me, so I continued: "You said that Albert went into the service when he was of age. That would have been when he was eighteen – so that would have been 1935. He didn't get out until the war was almost over, so that was almost ten years." I took a deep breath. What happened during that time, when he was in the service and you were still in Jackson Creek?"

Helena's smile faded noticeably, and her eyes took on a sad cast, but she nodded. "I had always thought Albert and I would marry, when I was in school. I thought that he would leave the army when his enlistment ran out, but right before then, the army started bringing in more men, because of what was happening overseas." She nodded again, and looked at each of us. "We never thought then that we might actually go to war, let alone how horrible that war would be. When the Germans ran through Poland and France as quickly as they did, I knew he might not get out of the army for some time." She looked at me again. "I realized he might not come home for years. He told me as much, when he came home for leave. He said there was talk of America having to help the British."

"So he stayed in the service," Stephanie said, "until 1945. You knew he would be away." She paused. "Did you meet someone else during that time?"

"Yes," Helena said. "Another boy from Jackson Creek, not quite as sweet and kind as Albert, but a good, strong man I knew I could count on. His name was Carl Pennington." She shook her head. "We married, and then he got drafted into the service in 1942, just before I learned we were going to have a child."

For a moment, none of us could speak. I looked from Stephanie to Steve; they both looked stunned. Helena gave us all a knowing look. "I can see this took you by surprise."

"Y-yes, ma'am," Stephanie managed to reply. "We just assumed from what you told us that you had married Albert."

"And I did," Helena answered. "Carl never came back from Europe – he died in France, a day or two after D-Day. A German sniper got him, they told me." She paused. "The baby – my daughter – was born dead, and just like that, I was all alone."

"I'm so sorry," I breathed. She waved her hand negligently at me.

"It was fifty years ago, now," she said. "Fifty years, and Albert came home less than a year later. He knew that I had gotten married, but he didn't know Carl had been killed, so it was a few weeks before ran into each other." Her smile bloomed again. "I wasn't sure Albert would want to be close to me again, but he understood, and it wasn't long before I was more in love with him than when we were in school.

"He loved me anyway, you see. He was a better man than I had thought, and once I knew that, I knew I'd never have anyone else but him." Her smile dimmed. "I just wish we'd had more time together, and that we could have had a child. After my little girl was born dead, the doctor told me he didn't think I could ever carry a child to term, and he proved to be right. I would have loved to have a little boy just like Albert."

I heard Stephanie take a deep breath, and knew what she was about to ask. I think everyone in the room did.

"Miss Helena, what happened on the night of the fire?" I heard her say.

Some of the light – a spark that had been in her eyes even when she spoke of the losses in her life – faded almost to nothing. Janie put her arm around her, and I said quietly, "If you don't want to talk about it, we understand."

"No." She shook her head almost defiantly, like a child being told to eat something nutritious, but unpleasant. "No, I want to tell this story. I want the people of that town to know the truth." She looked at us, with an expression that would have been angry if she hadn't been so much of a Southern lady. "Most of the whisperers and pointers are long gone now, and good riddance to them. But the younger folk, the ones who are getting older now, maybe they might learn something before they dry up and forget how to listen."

Stephanie's eyes widened, and she continued, "once you get on the wrong side of a town like that, their thinking, their mindset never changes. I saw it happen with other people. I never dreamed it would happen to me, until…" she bowed her head for a moment. Janie squeezed her gently.

"We know what it's like," I said. "If you're a misfit in any way, you're a second-class citizen. If the people in town think they have a reason to say bad things about you – whether it's true or not – they will."

Helena nodded, still staring into her lap, and then looked up at us again.

"Albert's older sister – Jane – was visiting us that night, with her boy Edward." she said. "Albert came home late from work – he had been up at the airstrip east of Stockville, fixing a crop duster – and he was tired, so after we had dinner, he said he needed to rest, so he went up to bed. Jane and I stayed in the downstairs parlor with Edward, talking and –" she made an odd face that I realized belatedly was, for want of a better word, naughty – "having an extra glass of wine.

"Jane and I were always good friends, and since she lived up in Toccoa – she married a railroad dispatcher who started in Jackson Creek, but was moved up to Toccoa during the Depression – we hardly got to see each other, maybe once or twice a year. So we were talking, and both feeling a little tipsy, I guess.

"We never smelled anything unusual. Albert would smoke a pipe sometimes, at the end of a long day, and I suppose that he dozed off in his chair, and dropped his pipe, but he was up in our bedroom and had closed the door, and cracked a window to let the smoke out. We never knew the place was on fire until we heard people shouting outside, and then heard pounding at the front door." Helena took a deep breath, leaning against Janie with her head in the hollow of her neck.

"There were two men and a teenager outside, and they dragged the three of us out. One of the men tried to go up the stairs, and we could hear shouting, but he came back out of the house alone. By the time the fire department came, the whole house had gone up." She heaved another sigh, shaking her head, and then sat up straight, almost defiantly.

"They told me later that Albert was gone before we even knew about the fire. There was so much smoke up there, even with the window cracked, that he probably never knew what was happening. I hoped they were right. I still do. I never saw him again, after he went up those stairs." She looked directly at me, then at Steve. "The VFW came to arrange his funeral. Jane was able to put me up in a motel until everything was done, and helped me with all the papers that had to be filled out and accounted for."

"Miss Helena, thank you for telling us all this," I managed to say. "Seeing how much this hurt you makes me wish we hadn't asked. I hope we can get the community to understand what really happened."

"It's all right," Helena said, more calmly. "I've lived with this ever since that day. It does help to talk about it now and then, even if it's hard to do."

Once we had gotten through that terrible day with her, the rest of her life's story was much less eventful. She had moved to Toccoa and lived with Jane, working as a secretary and a telephone operator until she was back on her feet. She moved to Lavonia in 1963 and began managing a diner there; she remained after retiring in 1984. The diner ("A place like Cleve's," Stephanie observed) had been successful enough that she could retire in some comfort.

It was almost noon by the time Helena finished her story, and we were all growing hungry, when an attendant arrived with a covered tray, which he set on the table beside her bed. She looked at Janie, then at me, and smiled.

"You all can go on, now. I know you're hungry, and you won't want to watch this old lady try to eat this meatloaf, or whatever it is today." She waved her hand at us again. "Go on."

Janie looked toward me, and nodded. We all stood, and Stephanie came over and gave her a gentle hug. "Thank you, Miss Helena," she said quietly.

"Thank you," I echoed her. Steve smiled at her, and she gave us another wave, and we filed out of her room, with Janie following behind.

CHAPTER FIVE

IT WAS A BIT complicated, figuring out how we would go to lunch. Steve wanted to go to the Waffle Grille, not that there were many other options; Janie had warned us off Helena's old diner, indicating that the place had declined badly after her aunt retired. In the end, Stephanie rode with Janie in her car – a clean, nondescript, fifteen-year-old Oldsmobile Delta 88 – and Steve rode with me.

"That was hard," Steve said as we turned out onto Parkertown Road. "I kind of feel bad that we asked her to re-live it all."

"Me, too," I replied. "Now we know exactly what happened, but I don't see how we can help Mr. Abbott. I mean, he's almost a hundred miles away, he hasn't seen her since he died, and if he's heard anything since, it's probably just been the same horrible rumors Miss Mollie and Ambrose told us about. Even if he learns the truth, it's not like he can get any sort of resolution from it."

"So we're at a… dead end," he said, a little sardonically. I glanced over at him.

"You might not want to make a joke like that in front of the girls," I warned. "Stephanie might not see the humor in it. Or Janie, for that matter."

Steve's grin was just slightly evil. "That's why I said it here."

The Waffle Grille was less than two miles from New Star. Janie followed us into the parking lot and parked beside us. I couldn't help noticing that her car was in really good shape, and as we went inside, I asked her about it.

"It was Helena's," she told me. "She had to stop driving when she moved into New Star, so she gave it to me. She bought it when I was in first grade. I remember she would never let me eat or drink anything in it."

"So she got it around 1982 or 1983." I glanced back at the car before going through the door. "Looks like it's about a 1977 or 1978."

"1978." Janie gave me a bit of a strange look as I followed her inside. Stephanie and Steve came in behind us.

"Good morning," one of the waitresses called to us from behind the bar. "Just get a table and someone will be right with you." A quick look around indicated that even though it was Saturday at lunchtime, business was slow, and we had our pick of almost any table.

With a meaningful glance at Steve, I led Janie to the right, until we were next to the door leading to the employees' area and restrooms. Steve went with Stephanie to the other end. I could see she was momentarily puzzled by this, but she didn't seem unhappy.

Janie and I sat down across from each other. Almost immediately, I became tongue-tied. As I had already noticed,

Janie was very pretty, and it seemed clear that she liked me – more, I realized, than Stephanie ever had, or at least that's how it seemed to me. I couldn't help smiling back at her, but I was still a little mystified.

Fortunately for me – or maybe she realized that she was going to have to – Janie spoke first, in a low voice: "When you called me, you asked me about my parents."

Oh. "Yes," I replied. "I have a feeling you're going to tell me something that's difficult to say."

"It sort of is," she answered. "Have you heard about the dam that broke and flooded the college near Toccoa?"

A chill ran down my backbone. I was pretty sure I knew where this was going to lead. "Steve's parents told him about it, when we first started planning to come up here," I answered. "I know it was in the seventies, and that it was really bad."

"It was." Janie hesitantly reached her hand across the table; I took it in mine. "My father was an instructor at the college – Toccoa Falls College. My grandmother told me that from the time he was a boy, he just seemed sure to grow up to be a minister, and he did. He started preaching in the local Baptist church when he was still a teenager, and went to seminary. Since my grandmother lived alone, he decided to try to find work as close to her as he could, and took a teaching job at the college.

"When the flood came, I was only a year old, so I don't remember any of it. My parents' house was destroyed, and they were caught in the wreckage. I was in my crib, and it somehow got loose from everything else and floated away in the flood. My grandmother said they found me half a mile from my house.

They said it was a miracle, that they found me like Moses in the bulrushes."

"I was afraid that you were going to tell me this," I said. I felt terrible for her, even though she remembered nothing of it. She smiled at me, a little sadly, but also with something else in her expression that took my breath away. Even Stephanie had never looked at me like that.

Just as I squeezed her hand, our waitress – Cassandra, her name tag read – appeared beside our table, and the moment vanished. "What'll you kids be having?" she asked absently, pen and pad in hand.

"I'll take the cheeseburger plate, and some sweet tea," I answered. She nodded, and looked toward Janie. "And you, dear?"

She thought for a moment. "Same thing, I guess," she answered.

"All right, babies. I'll have for you in just a minute." She moved away, barking out our order at the grillmaster. Janie smiled.

"I never even thought to look at the menu," she observed.

"Neither did I," I chuckled. "Good thing I knew what I wanted."

"I've only been here a few times," she said. "I live in Toccoa, with my grandmother. I'd like to take you to meet her, if that's OK."

"Sounds all right," I said. "We have a few hours before we have to go home. We have to drop Steve off in Tuckerton, and it's an hour from there to McDowell Mills, so we have to leave by about four-thirty. My folks are OK with me coming up, but they don't like me driving this far after dark."

"Sounds like my grandmother," she said. "But I only ever drive to school or to see Aunt Helena, so I'm usually back way before dark."

I was missing something, and finally, I figured out what it was. "Who do you hang out with, up here?" I asked. "Steve was in school with us last year, and he's a brainiac like the rest of our – our circle of friends, I guess you'd call it. But I really don't know much about you."

She shrugged. "I only have a few friends, and most of those I only see at school," she said. "My grandmother and I are Aunt Helena's only living relatives, and my grandmother's almost to the age where she'll need to be at New Star, too. I think she's only hanging on until I can get to college, and then she's going to have to have help, even if it's just someone coming by every day to check on her."

I felt guilty just for having friends. Janie was pretty much on her own. "How about school? I mean, what sort of courses are you taking?"

"I'm in the academic track," she said. "Our high school isn't great, but at least the advanced courses are good, and the kids who hate school the most drop out when they get to be sixteen or seventeen. My grandmother's said from the time I was little that I had to do well in school. I'll need a scholarship if I want to go to college."

I nodded. "Any idea what you want to do after college?" I asked.

"I don't really know," she answered. "I thought it might be interesting to study law, but I don't think I'd want to be an attorney. I'd like to do some writing, but I don't want to be a journalist." She paused. "Why do all the jerks take the interesting jobs?"

I had to laugh at that. "They must not find engineering or scientific research interesting. Even the jerks in those jobs are a lot more palatable, because they have to be able to back up what they say," I commented.

"Is that what you're interested in?" she asked. I shrugged.

"It's what I'm good at," I said. "Those jobs pay well, too. Well, engineering jobs, anyway." I grinned. "And academics may not make you rich, but unless you're really bad at it, it's pretty steady."

"So you don't have rich parents, either," she laughed. I shrugged again.

"Even if I did, the kind of jobs I'd like don't exist where I live," I said, and lowering my voice to a loud, conspiratorial whisper, I leaned across the table toward her and added, "and that's the biggest reason I'm interested in them. McDowell Mills sucks."

She had to laugh at that, and looking around, she mimicked my whisper. "Toccoa's not so great, either."

"What's so bad about it?" Cassandra had returned with our order. Janie's face flushed slightly as we both leaned back, and after our plates had been put on the table – none too gently, in Janie's case – we stopped talking for a few minutes as we ate. I hadn't realized how hungry I was.

"We'll need to tell Steve and Stephanie we're going to visit your grandmother," I finally said. She nodded, her mouth full, and I waited until she could answer. "It's almost twenty miles from here. If we leave now, we can get there before two," she said. She seemed about to say more, but stopped.

"OK," I said, a little uncertainly. I could see the same uncertainty in her expression as she smiled at me again.

TEN MINUTES LATER, the four of us were outside, working out the details of the trip to Janie's house. We agreed that we would split up as before, with Steve coming with me and Stephanie with Janie. We had barely pulled out of the parking lot before Steve began asking me about Janie.

"I mean, she obviously likes you," he said, as we drove north out of Lavonia into the foothill country - hills that became the Great Smokies not far beyond Toccoa Falls. "She's taking us to meet her family, so she has to at least want to date you, if that's even possible when you live so far apart."

"Steve, she doesn't really have much family," I answered, and took a deep breath. "Her mom and dad are dead. She lives with her grandmother. Helena is her only other living relative."

"What happened to her parents?" Steve asked. I glanced at him, and from his face, I could see he had already guessed the answer.

"They were killed in the flood in 1977," I said. "Her dad taught at the college. She was caught in the flood, too, but she survived."

"Wow." Steve didn't speak for a few minutes after that. We drove up State Highway 17 through a couple of old railroad towns that were barely more than wide places in the road; taken together, they weren't even a fourth as large as Lavonia, and Lavonia was barely the size of Jackson Creek. A few miles past them, the state highway made a left turn toward yet another town called Eastanollee. Janie continued north on Big A Road into Toccoa, and we followed.

Before long, we were in a Piedmont version of McDowell Mills. Much of the town appeared to be generational stores and businesses, but with a sprinkling of newer firms, with a couple of fast-food restaurants and a chain drugstore. Steve was shaking his head.

"This place is a hundred miles from Atlanta, and it's still more…" his voice trailed away, before he laughed. "I can't believe I'm using the word 'cosmopolitan,' but – yeah." He looked out the windshield from side to side, taking in the town as we drove through. "This place is actually more 'happening' than McDowell Mills." He looked at me again, with that same, slightly evil grin as earlier. "You know there's no excuse for your hometown, right?"

"Blame it on your uncle." I knew he was kidding, but if he was going to needle me, I was going to needle right back. He laughed again.

"That's fair," he said. "Though he did try to get rid of the worst parts of it."

"Maybe that's the difference," I answered. "Toccoa might just have had nicer people running it."

We fell silent again, as I followed Janie's Oldsmobile through the town until we reached Highway 284. She turned right, going more slowly up the two-lane road, and turned left onto Richmond Avenue, into a residential neighborhood eerily similar to the one surrounding New Star.

"Lost in the Fifties again," Steve commented.

Janie pulled into the fourth driveway on the left. Her house was a small, brick bungalow that looked as though it had been built – of course – around 1950. I parked my truck on the street in front of it as Stephanie and Janie got out of the Olds.

"My grandmother should be OK with you coming in," Janie called to me. "She's always worrying that I don't have enough friends."

"Let's hope so," Steve murmured. "Otherwise this could get really awkward, really fast."

Fortunately, Janie was right; from the moment we came in the house, her grandmother was nothing short of thrilled to see us. After a round of introductions – during which we learned that Janie had told her all about us, and that we were not, under any circumstances, to call her anything other than "Nana" – we found ourselves seated in her parlor. Her sofa and chairs seemed comfortable and the room was well appointed, if somewhat dated. I guessed that she had redecorated it some fifteen years before, just after the earth tones of the Woodstock era had gone out of style.

Nana bore a clear resemblance to her granddaughter, though her brown eyes and slightly more angular face were distinctly different. It was apparent Nana had once been, if not as pretty as Janie, very nearly so. They had similar smiles; Nana's was, if anything, even more welcoming than Janie's.

She had at first tried to press some refreshments on us, but relented when she realized we had just eaten, and instead asked me, "so how did you come to learn about our family? None of us has lived anywhere near McDowell Mills since my brother passed, and that was over thirty years ago."

We looked at each other. Nana was watching me expectantly; it seemed Janie had told her more about me than

Steve or Stephanie. I felt flattered, even though I was a bit nervous.

"We're part of the high school's Historical Society," I said after a moment's hesitation. "McDowell Mills is starting to change, because Atlanta has gotten so large. We've been trying to put together a sort of slice of life in the town, for each generation we can. Where people are still living, we try to interview them and learn what their lives were like, and when they're not, we can try to track down their relatives."

"We found out that the cemetery at First New Jerusalem Methodist is really… odd," Stephanie put in. "It was a new church back in the 1940s, and it sort of turned into a catch-all for people who had died and weren't – weren't exactly welcome in the in-town cemeteries. Some of the people there are sort of local legends. We learned about one – a girl named Sarah Beckwith – who died in 1953 under mysterious circumstances. We were able to find out the truth of what happened to her.

"After that, we just started looking for other people buried there who had unusual circumstances surrounding their deaths, and we came across Albert Abbott." Stephanie paused. "It took almost a month for us to find where Helena had gone, and even then, we were lucky to find her. We had to go through the state tax rolls."

Steve glanced at her. "So that's how you found her," he said. "I hadn't known that."

"Well, you had already moved back to Tuckerton," she replied, very slightly tartly. Nana's eyebrows raised in amusement.

"And what was the story in McDowell Mills, about how my brother passed?" she asked.

"That was the point," I answered her. "We couldn't get a clear story. There were some people who blamed Helena for the fire, but none of them were there or saw what happened, and that kind of rumor's what people in McDowell Mills live for. The most reliable sources we could find all said it appeared to be an accident, but that Helena left almost as soon as the funeral was over, and never came back. The scandal-mongers took that as proof."

Nana's lips pressed tightly together for a moment. "You know now, of course, that that wasn't true at all."

"Yes, ma'am," I said hurriedly. "None of us believed the rumors. We know what that place can be like. We just wanted to have the whole story, so that we could set the record straight."

Nana nodded at this, then glanced toward Janie. "Neither of us ever went back there after the funeral. Some of the ruder folks there didn't even have the decency to be quiet about what they thought. Helena was just devastated – she lost everything – and here were some of the worst people I've ever met or even heard of, whispering about how she'd done it on purpose," she almost hissed. "We all grew up in Jackson Creek, so we weren't really McDowell Mills people – and of course, they assumed the worst."

"We know," Stephanie said. "It's starting to change, but not fast enough for me to stay. I want out as soon as I finish school."

"Me too," I said. Janie smiled at me again.

"Well, that's probably for the best, then," Nana said. "Will you be staying to supper?"

"We can't, really," Stephanie answered. "It's three hours home from here, and we promised Chad's mom that he'd be home before dark."

"Well, that's a shame," Nana said. "Next time you're in town, come here for lunch. I'll take good care of you."

"Thanks, Nana," Steve replied.

WE SPENT ANOTHER hour there, talking. Nana wanted to know everything about each of us – our families, what we wanted to do after school, what sort of music we liked – literally everything. I was floored by the revelation that she loved grunge rock, and thought the rockabilly music from the fifties should have been left there – "buried in an unmarked grave," as she put it – once the Beatles emerged. She grilled me a little harder than Steve and Stephanie, to the point that they were hard-pressed not to reveal their amusement. Janie clearly had been talking with her about me.

It was nearing three o'clock when Janie stood, saying to Nana, "There's one place I need to show them before they go back home." She looked meaningfully at each of us. "You'll be coming back to visit soon, won't you?"

"I will be, for sure." The words were out of my mouth before I knew it. Knowing grins bloomed across Steve and Stephanie's faces, but Janie's corresponding smile made it worth the ribbing I would no doubt be taking later.

"We'll all keep in touch," Stephanie added. "Maybe you could come down for a weekend and stay with us."

Janie looked to Nana, who smiled. "I'm sure that will be fine."

We said our goodbyes, and left. Janie signaled for me to follow her as she went back toward Big A Road, where she turned right. "You notice something about Nana?" Steve asked me, as we followed her.

I thought about that. "Her favorite music," I finally answered. "She was like us, growing up, I'd bet."

"Yeah," Steve answered. "And she grew up in Jackson Creek, probably in the Thirties, when the Depression was. I bet Toccoa seemed like paradise by comparison."

A HALF MILE AHEAD, the road ended in a T-intersection, and Janie turned left, going north. Another half mile later, she slowed, turning into a large cemetery that had been built around a low hill.

I glanced toward Steve after turning into the cemetery. "She's taking us to her parents' graves," I said. He didn't reply, and I realized he was looking around, scanning the memorials.

"You think we might see ghosts here?" I asked.

"Anything's possible," he replied. "You guys taught me that."

We crested the hill. Janie had stopped about fifty yards ahead of us; I eased my truck up behind her car, and shut off the engine. Janie and Stephanie had already gotten out, and were walking downhill to the right of the car path. They came to a halt near a memorial plaque set in the ground, which had a small bouquet of wildflowers in its installed vase. Steve and I came up beside her. Almost without thinking about it, I put an arm around Janie's shoulder, and she sighed, leaning against me.

The plaque was like all the others around it; the cemetery had some older sections which still featured gravestones, but where we stood, almost every memorial was flat on the ground. The marker read:

SAWYER

EDWARD HUBERT	**ROBERTA BROWN**
JULY 31, 1949	**OCTOBER 7, 1950**
NOVEMBER 6, 1977	**NOVEMBER 6, 1977**

They weren't much older than we were, I realized. I wondered briefly how I would respond if I found out I only had ten years to live, and that moment of distraction kept me from noticing something else. It wasn't until I saw Stephanie nudge Steve that I followed her eyes. I blinked, and realizing what it was, I looked back down at Janie. We were all looking at the same thing.

A young couple was walking across the cemetery toward us from the woods at its northern end. They were dressed conservatively, and rather plainly; he was stoop-shouldered and sandy-haired, wearing a white, button-down shirt and a sport jacket with collar points that were entirely too wide, and starched slacks. She was brunette and slightly mousy-looking, clad in a white sundress that was very slightly too large for her. Knowing that he had been a pastor, I was taken a bit aback; it took a few moments for me to remember that their home had been destroyed in the flood, and it was likely even the clothes they wore at burial were given to them as a last act of charity.

They were both fairly plain-looking; clearly, Nana's good looks had skipped his generation. Both of them seemed innocuous, but strangely wary. It occurred to me that Janie probably had never brought anyone else here – at least not recently – other than Nana; the cemetery was close enough to her house that she could have walked there, in the years before she learned to drive.

"You come here a lot, don't you?" I asked her quietly. She looked up at me for a moment, and I knew right then that she thought she was the only one who could see them.

"It's all of my parents that I have," she finally said. I felt a lump in my throat. She had brought us here so that her parents could see us, even though she thought we couldn't see them. It became clear to me why she had so few friends: very probably, sometime in the past, she had brought someone to meet them – only then realizing no one else could see them. She would have been marked, almost from the time she began school, as one of the weird kids. Someone who didn't fit in.

Someone like us.

"Janie," I whispered. She didn't move. Her parents – Edward and Roberta – had stopped some ten feet away from us. They looked over Steve and Stephanie, before focusing on me; their expressions were nonplussed.

"Janie, there's a man and a woman standing just on the other side of the marker," I whispered. She gasped, and looked at me with the same mistrust that I saw in her eyes when we'd first met at New Star. I looked back at her parents again. "He's wearing a button-down shirt and jacket, and she's wearing a dress that doesn't quite fit right."

The mistrust vanished, and tears sprang in her eyes. "Please tell me you're not making this up."

"Hello, Pastor Sawyer, Mrs. Sawyer," Steve said, lifting a hand in greeting. A small, surprised smile crept into the faces of both ghosts, and they waved back.

"He's raising his left hand. She's waving with her right. They're both smiling," I said quietly.

Her eyes met mine again – and all of her worry, mistrust, and fear had vanished. The next thing I knew, she was hugging me so hard that I could barely breathe. She pulled back from me for a moment, and then kissed me so emphatically that I was nearly knocked over – and that was just the physical force of her kiss. All at once, she disengaged, and hugged first Stephanie, then Steve, nearly as powerfully as she had me.

Pastor Sawyer spoke. His voice had a slightly airy quality, yet was rich and clear. He probably had been an excellent singer when he was alive; for all I knew, he might still be. "For all these years, our little girl thought she might have something wrong with her," he said. "She could see us, when no one else could."

"We can see you," Steve said. "Obviously. Where we come from, there's a cemetery full of – of people like you. We've been trying to learn more about who they are, and why…" his voice trailed away.

"Why they're like we are," her mother said, with an understanding smile. "We had to know that our daughter would be happy, so we stayed to be sure."

"She's been able to see us from the time she was little," Pastor Sawyer added. "So much so, that we couldn't stay around my mother's house. She was already starting to worry about Janie, by the time she was three, so we came here. We thought that she would grow up, and forget us, but instead, she came to see us as often as she could."

I looked at Janie again. Her eyes were streaming tears, but she was smiling, and she nodded agreement to what her father had said.

"Still, we worried for her, because she was almost alone growing up," her mother continued. "We had to be sure that she wouldn't always be alone. She brought her little friends here a few times, years ago, but none of them could see us, and after a while, she didn't have any friends close enough to bring here. You three are the first we've met since she was ten years old."

"So you could have left at any time?" I heard myself ask.

"Not while she was alone," Pastor Sawyer replied. "But she's not alone any more, and when it's time, we can go in peace."

"And when will that be?" Stephanie asked. Janie looked apprehensively at her.

"When it's time for her to leave home," her father replied simply. "We were meant to live in Toccoa Falls, but Janie isn't. The day will come for her to spread her wings, and when she leaves, we will fly away as well."

"That's why we came here," I said without thinking. The stunned expression Janie gave me, and the surprised looks I received from Pastor and Mrs. Sawyer, reminded me that none of them knew about Mr. Abbott. I exchanged a glance with Steve, and said, "Janie, we didn't say so before, because we had the same problem you did – we didn't know if you would believe us when we told you, but now we know you will."

"We went looking for Helena because we – we've seen her husband, Albert, in the cemetery in McDowell Mills," Steve added. "Your uncle," he said, motioning toward Pastor Sawyer. He looked astonished.

"I remember my uncle, just a little bit," he said slowly. "My mother took me to visit him when I was five, and one time he and Aunt Helena came to visit us here in Toccoa. He was a mechanic, I think."

"That's right," Stephanie said. "He died in 1957. Their house burned down."

"I remember that as well," Pastor Sawyer said. "Aunt Helena came to live with us for two or three years after that. Mama said she'd lost everything in the fire."

Stephanie's voice was thick with tears as she spoke. "We left some flowers on his grave last week. I don't know if anyone's visited it in years. He looked really touched."

"I've never been there," Janie said. "I know neither Helena nor Nana ever went back. They grew up in Jackson Creek, so they wouldn't have had any reason to go to McDowell Mills, except to visit him."

I looked from Pastor Sawyer to his wife, then down at Janie again. "Your great-uncle is still here for a reason, but we don't know why. I don't know if anyone has ever asked him. The problem is, Helena probably isn't up to traveling, so we can't bring her there, and we wouldn't know if she could see him, even if we did."

"There was someone else we met in that cemetery," Steve said. "Sarah told us that she couldn't ride in a car – she had to walk. So we can't bring either of them to meet the other."

Pastor Sawyer and his wife looked at each other. "We can't ride in cars, either. We learned that when Janie was still a baby."

"It's getting late," Stephanie said. "We'll have to leave soon, but I promise, we'll try to figure this out."

"There's no hurry," Mrs. Sawyer said, without irony. "Time moves differently for us. You'll find a way."

Janie leaned into me again, and I hugged her close for a moment. When we disengaged, she looked back to her parents once more. "Bye, Mama. Bye, Daddy," she whispered, waving. They waved back, not only to her, but to each of us, and then faded out.

It was like waking from a dream, but with Janie beside me, it was like the dream had become real. She was smiling at me, even though a tear had trailed down her cheek. Steve and Stephanie were walking back toward our cars, hands clasped. I sighed, knowing we had to leave.

She gave me one more quick kiss, then seized my hand and pulled me along, back to my truck. "You really want me to go, right now?" I asked her.

"I want you to get home on time, so that you can come back here next week," she answered. Steve and Stephanie both snorted, almost identically, and climbed in as Janie guided me – rather forcefully – to the driver's side door, and gave me a look that expected no opposition. I shrugged, but before I got in, I kissed her one last time.

She broke the kiss before I would have liked. "Get in," she said, bumping my shoulders with her palms. She was smiling, but she meant it, and with another shrug, I did as she demanded. As I put the keys in the ignition, about to start the engine as I watched Janie walk toward her vast Oldsmobile, Steve commented: "Where's Mr. Singer when we need him?"

Even I had to laugh at that, remembering Steve's first kiss with Stephanie, as I followed Janie out of the cemetery.

CHAPTER SIX

WE HAD ONE MORE week of summer left to us when we returned. I had to mow the lawn that Sunday, and I needed some new clothes and supplies for school, but I was able to call Steve late that afternoon.

Almost as soon as he answered the phone, he spoke without preamble. "We're going to have to talk to Mr. Abbott this week."

"I know. I just don't know if he'll talk to us," I answered. "I think Stephanie should be the one who tells him. He may not even know about Janie, or that his nephew and his wife are dead."

I hadn't thought of that. "Whatever we do, we probably need to figure it out this week," I finally said. "Once school starts, it's going to be a lot harder to go back and forth. It's six hours just driving, and that doesn't leave much time for visiting."

"Or dating," Steve added. "It's difficult enough just going back and forth to McDowell Mills, and that's less than an hour. It's worth it, for sure, but having to go that far, and having to get back before too late, that'd be tough. Have you talked to her since you got back?"

"Not yet," I said. I was trying to make sure I didn't call her too often. It was long-distance from McDowell Mills to Toccoa, and though it wasn't all that expensive, I wanted to make sure it didn't get that way. Running up a fifty-dollar phone bill would have gotten me in hot water really fast. Since Nana was obviously on Social Security, I was reasonably sure Janie would understand if I didn't call every day. I had already written her a letter, telling her a little more about myself, but I would have much preferred seeing her in person.

Steve read my mind. "Long distance, eh? Just another thing to put up with, at least for a year. You talk about where you're going after graduation?"

I hadn't said anything about that, but I had already thought about studying engineering. My first choice had been Georgia Tech, but after meeting Janie, Clemson was looking a lot more interesting. I had sent off for an application and for financial aid information, just in case.

"I'm thinking about Clemson," I answered. "And Tech, obviously. It's kind of early to be narrowing down on a college."

"No, it isn't," Steve said. "You should already be getting your applications in."

"I meant that it's a little early to be making decisions like that with Janie in mind," I answered. "I mean, sure, we like each other, but we'd have to make it through senior year."

"That's true." Steve paused, and I could tell he was uncomfortable when he asked, "Do you feel the same way about Janie that you did about Stephanie?"

I had to laugh a little. "Not even close. Stephanie and I have been friends for years. Dating for us was like trying on a shirt to see if it fit. It didn't, so everything was OK, and when she met you, all I wanted was the best for her. For both of you, once we became friends."

"OK. Good." He paused again. "I guess we know now why someone as pretty as Janie is, would be as alone as she says she is. Between Nana, Helena and her parents, she must seem really weird to people who live in Toccoa."

"It's not just Toccoa," I pointed out. "She'd be a misfit anywhere. She'd be in our crowd, if she lived here."

"That's true," Steve said again. "Maybe that's part of being able to see ghosts. You have to see how everyone lives from the outside – the way they probably see us."

"I dunno." I thought for a few seconds. "I'm going to call her tomorrow, and start planning for this weekend. It'll be my last chance to see her before school starts back."

"Good idea. Want us to come too?"

I hesitated. "If you want to. I think Janie and I would like some time by ourselves, though."

"Oh, I get that, totally," Steve answered. "Remember the bowling alley?"

I laughed aloud. It had taken Steve weeks to kiss Stephanie, and he had had to get her into the bowling alley parking lot in Jackson Creek to be alone with her. "Want me to ask Mr. Singer to come along?"

He started laughing as well. "Maybe he and Miss Roberts could make it a date, too."

The image of the two of them – prim Miss Roberts and loud Mr. Singer – on a date together had us laughing for some time. "I'll have to keep that in mind. I wonder if Miss Roberts has ever even been on a date," I finally managed to say.

"I wonder if Mr. Singer has," Steve responded, and we were laughing again.

THE FOLLOWING EVENING, I was just finishing the dishes and getting ready to call Janie when our phone rang. My mom answered, and her eyebrows lifted in surprise as she looked over at me. "I'll get him. One second." She handed the phone to me, still looking bemused. "It's a girl, but it's not Stephanie," she said.

I was a little anxious as I took the phone from her, hoping Janie wasn't upset with me for not calling yet. "Hi Janie. I was just about to call you."

She didn't answer for a moment. I could hear her breathing, but it sounded wrong. "Janie, are you all right?" I asked.

"No. No, I'm not." She gave a slight, gasping sob. She was starting to cry.

"Janie, what's happened? Is it Nana?" I asked, suddenly very worried.

"No." Another sob. "It's Aunt Helena," she finally managed to say. "They think she's had a heart attack. They took her to the hospital about an hour ago."

"Oh, no!" I said, stricken. "Where's the hospital?"

"It's just up the road from the cemetery, almost to Toccoa Falls," she managed to answer. "They took her there just a little while ago. Nana and I are about to go up there."

"OK. Go, then. Let me know what's going on as soon as you can." I swallowed. I didn't want my parents to see how upset I was, and I could only imagine how Janie felt. She only had two living relatives, and one was in real danger. "I'm so sorry, Janie. Do you need for me to come up there?"

"Not yet," she answered. "I'll call you when I know. It might be tomorrow."

"All right. Just go be with her and Nana." I paused. In that moment I wanted to tell her I loved her, just as a reassurance, but it wasn't the time. I think she knew anyway.

"Thank you, Chad. Bye." She hung up without waiting for an answer. I looked over to see my mom watching me.

"Whoever that was, something bad's happened," she said. "Is this girl from up in north Georgia?"

"Yes, she is," I managed to say. Mom looked both sympathetic and reproving – a very Mom look.

"Is she the real reason you've gone up there the last two weeks?" she asked.

"No, Mom," I managed to answer. "The man we were trying to learn more about – Albert Abbott – had a wife named Helena. She was in a nursing home in Lavonia, so we went there to visit her and learn more about him."

I described the interviews with Helena, and how we met Janie, and how Janie and I had clicked almost from the beginning. I left off the kissier parts, but I think she got the general idea of what was going on.

"So Janie called to tell me that Helena's had a heart attack, and they've taken her to the hospital," I finished. "She said she would call me as soon as she knew what was going on."

"And what do her parents think of all this?" she asked.

"She lives with her grandmother," I replied. "Her parents were killed in the flood in Toccoa when she was a baby."

Mom's face softened. "Poor thing," she breathed. "And now she might lose her aunt. Does she have any other family?"

"No. At least, I don't think so," I said. "Everyone in that family – both families, the Abbotts and Helena's – they're all gone, as far as I know. Nana's the only one that's left."

Mom looked nearly as upset as I felt when she said that. "Does she need for you to go up there?" she asked.

"Not yet," I answered. "But I think she will – on Saturday, if not before then."

"Just tell me when you need to go," she said. "Has she been down here to visit yet?"

"Not yet," I said. "Stephanie's already said Janie could stay with her, but with Helena sick, Nana would be left alone. I don't know whether Janie would want that."

Mom nodded. "All right. Just keep me posted." She paused. "I'm sorry, Chad."

"So am I, Mom," I answered. I swallowed again. "I have to tell Steve and Stephanie."

"All right," Mom said. She left the kitchen, and I quickly called first Stephanie, and then Steve. Stephanie was deeply upset – as much as I was – but I knew that was how she would react. It was Steve who pointed something out that I'd missed.

"What do we do about Mr. Abbott?" he asked me, after I had filled him in. "How are we going to be able to help him out? And if Helena doesn't make it – what happens then?"

I hadn't thought about that. Steve always seemed to catch on a little quicker to what the ghosts needed, and I realized that without Helena, Mt. Abbott might not have anywhere left to go.

"We need to meet, tomorrow, and we need to visit Mr. Abbott again. If nothing else, we need to tell him what's happened. He might be able to tell us something, or might know what to do." I paused. "Can you call Stephanie for me? I just talked to her, and she's pretty upset. She probably needs to hear from you."

"Sounds good. Stockville again, tomorrow at eight?" he asked.

"Yeah," I said. "But we should still go to Cleve's some, at least until they go under."

"You really think that'll happen?" Steve asked. "There'll be more places to eat, sure, but there's going to be a lot more people there. Besides, you know how the good-old-boy network can be. They'll want to keep things the way they always have been."

"True, but still – remember how much less crowded it was last time?" I pointed out. Steve sighed.

"I guess we'll find out eventually. Anyway, we'll talk tomorrow."

After we hung up, I went out of the kitchen and up to my room, still worrying about Janie and Mr. Abbott, and not sure what to do about either.

THE NEXT MORNING, the three of us met at Bryan's. I didn't think I would be very hungry – I'd slept badly, worrying about everyone affected by Helena's condition, including Helena herself – but once I smelled breakfast, I ended up piling a plate high with eggs, bacon, gravy, grits and biscuits. Stephanie stared in surprise at my heaping mountain of food.

"Sorry. I didn't know I was this hungry until I got here." I attacked my plate as Stephanie glanced toward Steve, who said, "We're going to have to tell Mr. Abbott about Helena. Have you heard back from Janie yet?"

"Not yet," I mumbled through a mouthful of food. I finished chewing, swallowed, and said, "My mom gave me the go-ahead to drive up there if anything else happens."

"My parents said I could go, too," Stephanie said.

"Same here," Steve added. I nodded, and shoveled more food into my mouth. They both watched me chewing, until I swallowed again and said, "We need to get going. We'll have to get more flowers for Mr. Abbott's grave, at the least. We know that should get his attention."

Steve shrugged. "I guess you're right," Stephanie said.

We ate quickly and in near silence after that. Twenty minutes and a second plate later, I was back in my truck, and Steve and Stephanie were following me to Miss Mollie's. I hoped she opened at nine; if not, we would have to find some other way to pass the time until then.

Fortunately, Mollie's shop had opened by the time we arrived. Ambrose was at a table in the middle of the store, working on a small flower arrangement; he glanced up and smiled. "And what would you three be wanting to ask about today?" he asked in his deep, warm voice.

"No questions today. We just need another flower arrangement for Mr. Abbott," Stephanie said. Ambrose looked surprised.

"I thought for sure you'd be asking about some other poor soul you'd come across," he said. "Do you mind my asking what you learned about Mr. Abbott?"

Steve looked oddly at me. "We learned most of his life history," I replied. "We did locate his family, and we talked with his widow for some time."

He studied each of us in turn, nodding slowly. "And did you learn any more about the, ah, circumstances of his passing?" he asked.

"We're positive Helena – Mrs. Abbott – didn't do it,' I said.

"Helena thought that Albert dozed off with a lit pipe," Steve put in. "She was in the house with her sister when the fire started."

Ambrose nodded thoughtfully. "Pure curiosity, of course. One hears many stories in a town like this. Sometimes, they even prove to be true, if the people doing the deeds are worse than the people passing the rumors."

"Helena's sweet," Stephanie said thickly. She was getting emotional again. "She talked with us for hours about him, and about their life together. She said she's never come back here since then."

"Understandable," Ambrose replied thoughtfully. "So what sort of arrangement will you want for Mr. Abbott?"

"How about a half-dozen chrysanthemums?" Steve asked. "With some other flowers, of course."

Ambrose smiled, his teeth surprisingly white and near-perfect. "I believe I know what you have in mind. I'll have that ready for you momentarily."

As Ambrose moved about the store assembling the arrangement for Mr. Abbott, I looked over at Steve. "What was that look all about?" I asked.

"Ambrose knew more than he let on," Steve said in a low voice. "He probably knew about Carl Pennington, and about Helena's baby."

I considered that for a few seconds. "He would have been too young to know about that, but Mollie might have heard something," I said. "Maybe. But I had thought they were still in Jackson Creek when she married him."

Steve shrugged. "Maybe it was like the fire," he said. "All that anyone would know was that she had a baby that died, and the father wasn't around. That's all the people in McDowell Mills would need to know, or would bother finding out. Back then, she would have been shunned on general principle."

"True," I conceded. "Not that they needed much reason to shut her out. As bad as it is now, it must have been twice as bad then."

Ambrose had moved back behind the store curtain. As we made our way to the counter at the rear of the shop, we could hear him speaking to Mollie, but what he said was unintelligible. A few minutes later, he emerged with Mr. Abbott's flowers, contained in a plastic vase with water in it, and wrapped loosely around in gold-edged cellophane.

"Ambrose?" Stephanie asked hesitantly. He turned his tolerant smile toward her, his eyebrows slightly lifted in anticipation of her question. She continued, "Were you expecting us to ask about Helena's baby?"

Ambrose's brows lifted slightly higher. "So you know about that. My mother told me a few things about the Abbotts after you left last time. I confess I wondered whether she had told you about that."

"She did," Steve said. He seemed very slightly on edge; I could tell he thought Ambrose might have heard the town gossips' version of events – whatever that was. "Mr. Abbott went into the Army in 1935 and served through the war. While he was in the Army, Helena stayed in Jackson Creek, and married a man named Carl Pennington. He went into the service in 1942, about the same time as Helena realized she was pregnant, and he died during the invasion of France after D-Day."

"So she was a war widow," Ambrose intoned softly. "And the baby?"

"Her baby was stillborn," Stephanie said. "She wasn't ever able to have another one."

Ambrose nodded thoughtfully. "And without benefit of the full story, that would have been enough to set tongues wagging," he said.

"How much of this did you already know?" Steve asked. He was trying to hide it, but I could see that something in Ambrose's responses had angered him. The florist lifted a placating hand.

"Very little. Even my mother only knew about the baby's death, and that the baby's mother wasn't married," he said. "I was unaware that she had married once before she married Albert Abbott."

"It seems no one in McDowell Mills knew about it," I said, glancing toward Steve and hoping he wouldn't express what was in his mind. "Miss Helena talked with us twice, for a couple of hours each time. She told us a lot about herself and Mr. Abbott, but she never mentioned any friends here – only the ones she had in Jackson Creek when she was a girl. The man she married was from Jackson Creek."

"My mother said that there were rumors about the Abbotts," Ambrose replied in his patient voice. "They had no children, and they kept to themselves for the most part. But she also said that she had never heard anything definite about them – just rumors, and those are a dime a dozen here." He sighed. "It's good that you're getting to the bottom of stories like hers. Truth and light dispel lies and darkness, and this town's seen more than enough of those."

Steve nodded, and I could see the tension in his expression ease. "That's how we feel about it, too," he replied.

We paid for the flowers – or at least, Steve did – and thanked Ambrose for his help. We climbed back into our trucks and pulled out onto Speedway Road, then turned left onto Highway 255 toward the library, and beyond that, New Jerusalem. The library was still closed when we passed it – it didn't open until ten – but we had planned to go straight to the cemetery in any case.

Ten minutes later, we had parked at the cemetery fence and climbed out. The sky was overcast, and the morning was cooler than was usual for summer. Once we got around the fence, Stephanie carried the flowers, with Steve and myself flanking her.

We reached the grave. The flowers we had left before had wilted, so Steve removed them from their container, and Stephanie moved the new ones to the vase built into Albert's marker. We stepped back a couple of paces from the plaque, uncertain of what to expect.

"He usually only comes up at sunset," Stephanie whispered. Steve glanced at her with an odd smile.

"Why are you whispering? Are you afraid you'll wake him up?" he asked. She shot him a dark look, then turned to face us.

"I know, we *want* him to wake up, but I don't want to offend him," she said. Her annoyance faded into puzzlement when she saw that Steve and I were both grinning.

"He's behind me, isn't he?" she asked, with another dark look for us to share.

"I'm not offended," came an unfamiliar, surprisingly warm voice from behind her, she turned and saw Mr. Abbott standing about six feet from her, on the other side of his gravesite. He was smiling – the first time any of us had ever seen him do so – and it was clear he was as amused as the rest of us were.

"Thank you for the flowers. No one had ever left any there, until you did," he said. His voice was a little higher than I would have expected, but clear and strong; like his nephew, he had probably been a good singer.

"You're – you're welcome," Stephanie replied, clearly flustered.

"Tell me, why did you leave them? You didn't place any on the other markers. Why did you choose me?" His face was honestly inquisitive.

We looked at each other, hesitating, before Stephanie answered, "we found out where Helena went after she left, and talked with her. There was a horrible story being told about her starting the fire, and the people here were so awful to her, that as soon as your funeral was over, she left with her sister and never came back."

"So she's in Toccoa?" Mr. Abbott asked.

"She was, until she had to go to a – a nursing home," I said. I didn't know if he'd understand what an "assisted living facility" was. "She was in Lavonia until yesterday."

"Until yesterday." He thought about that for a moment. "Has she died?"

"Not yet," Stephanie said, her voice thickening with emotion. "She had a heart attack, and she's in the hospital in Toccoa."

"I see," Mr. Abbott said softly. He turned and began walking away from us, toward the highway.

"Wait!" Steve said. He paused, and looked back at us over his shoulder.

"Where are you going?" I asked.

"To be with my wife, if she's still alive when I get there," he said, a trace of bitterness in his voice.

"Then there's something we should tell you," Steve said. "Your sister's still in Toccoa, at her old house. Her granddaughter is the only other living relative she has."

Mr. Abbott's expression was one of surprised sadness. "My sister Jane had a son," he said. "My nephew, Edward. He was still a baby when his father was killed in Korea. He was only eight when…" his voice trailed away, then returned, more sharply. "What happened to him?"

"He grew up and got married, and had a little girl," I answered. "Her name's Janie. Edward was a teacher at the college in Toccoa Falls, until he was killed in the flood there in

1977. His wife died in the same flood. Janie survived, and grew up in your sister's house."

Mr. Abbott's face was so saddened, and so desolate, that Stephanie took a step toward him. "I'm sorry we had to tell you all this," she said. "We know she didn't set the fire that – that –" She couldn't finish the sentence.

"It's all right," he answered. "When I woke up – like this – it was almost a day later," he said. "The house was completely destroyed – so much so that nothing was salvageable. I didn't know what to do, so I looked around town until I learned where my funeral would be.

"I tried to speak to Helena, to try to comfort her, but she couldn't see or hear me. She was disconsolate. Even at the funeral, she always had her hands over her face." His voice became bitter. "I could hear the whisperings from some of the townsfolk. They said terrible things about her, and I couldn't do anything to stop them."

"Most people can't see you," I said. "We don't really know why we can. But Janie, your niece, can see – people like you. She can see her parents."

As I said this, Mr. Abbott's expression suddenly became hopeful. "Do you think she could see me?" he asked.

"We don't know," Stephanie replied, and Steve added, "we saw her parents when we visited her on Saturday. She – she was going to visit them, and just pretend to be showing us their graves, but then she found out we could see them as she could."

"If I were to go up there, do you think she could get a message to Helena?" he asked. We all looked at each other again.

"I'm sure she could," I finally replied. "If she can see you. We didn't see any other ghosts there, so we can't say for sure that she will be able to."

Mr. Abbott studied each of us for a few seconds. "Then I will need for you to go visit her, in a day or two," he said quietly. "I will travel to Toccoa, to the hospital, and wait there." He started to turn away again.

"How will you get there?" Stephanie called after him. He glanced back over his shoulder.

"I'll walk," he replied.

"But that's ninety miles, or more," Stephanie protested. "That'll take days."

Mr. Abbott gave us an odd smile before he turned again and continued walking away. As he left, we heard him say, "It's not as though I have anything better to do."

CHAPTER SEVEN

JANIE CALLED ME early Wednesday morning, shortly after I got up. Her news wasn't good.

"She's in a coma," she told me, her voice breaking. "The doctors don't know whether she'll ever wake up again."

I felt terrible for her. "We told her husband what happened," I heard myself say. "He's walking there now. He'll probably get there sometime late this afternoon."

"He's walking?" she asked. "All that way?"

"There's no other way for him to get there," I answered. "He didn't even know what happened to your mom and dad. He did ask whether we thought you'd be able to see him, and then asked whether we would be going back up there.."

"Will you be able to come back here today?" she asked.

"I think so," I answered. "My parents know what happened, and how serious it is. I think they'll let me go. Do you want me to bring Steve and Stephanie?"

"Yes." She paused for a moment. "If they can come. I need all the friends I can get right now, and I think Nana would be glad to have you here, too."

"Just sit tight," I told her. "I'll call them and make sure it's OK, and then I'll be on my way."

I got up and went into the kitchen. Mom was already making breakfast for Dad before he left for work, and when she looked up at me, she knew right away what was going on.

"How's your girlfriend doing?" she asked. I wasn't entirely sure she was my girlfriend – at least not yet – but I let that pass. If that got me to Toccoa faster, then it was fine by me.

"Not good," I answered her. "Her aunt's in a coma and the doctors don't know if she's going to recover. She asked if we could come up to see her today."

I had expected her to check with my dad, or just think about it for a minute, but her answer was immediate. "Your dad and I discussed this last night. We decided you can go, as long as you're back before nine tonight."

"OK. Thanks, Mom." I picked up the telephone and called Stephanie – fortunately, she was awake – and let her know I was coming to pick her up; I called Steve right after, and then called Janie back. She still sounded upset, of course, but also grateful that we were coming.

I PICKED UP STEVE at his house a little more than an hour later. "Traffic may be bad," he warned me. "We're going against it once we get on the interstate, but it's usually kind of crowded getting there this time of day." He wasn't wrong – it took nearly twenty minutes to drive the three miles from his house to the freeway, and until we had gotten about fifteen miles north, there was still a lot of traffic. Once it began to thin out, the drive up was as uneventful as before, but the worry we all felt for Helena – and for Nana and Janie – made it seem a lot longer.

"You remember how to get there?" Steve asked, as we finally left the interstate in Lavonia. I steered the truck left, toward Toccoa.

"I'll take us to Nana's first. If nobody's there, we'll go to the hospital," I answered.

We reached Nana's house a little while after ten. Janie's car wasn't in the driveway, so I turned the truck around, and went back to the main road, heading for the cemetery.

"The hospital's just past the cemetery," I told Steve and Stephanie as I turned off Tugalo Street – Big A Road changed names just before the turn to go to their house – onto Broad Street, and then went left onto Falls Road toward the cemetery. As we passed it, I couldn't help glancing out to see whether any ghosts were visible, but none were evident.

"I wonder whether there's any other ghosts there," I commented as we left the cemetery behind. Neither of them answered, and only a minute later, we saw a sign indicating the left turn for the hospital. A stone sign on our right announced Toccoa Falls College. I saw Steve fidgeting uncomfortably as we passed it; not a hundred yards ahead, another sign on the left indicated Stephens County Hospital.

We turned, following the road through the hospital complex. I was relieved to see that it was a reasonably large building, almost a hundred yards across and three stories tall; the hospital in Jackson Creek was tiny, and I had worried that we might find something similar there. There was a parking lot on our left that was about two-thirds full; as we pulled in, I noticed Janie's Delta 88 parked in the row nearest the hospital.

"Helena must have been brought in after hours," Steve observed. There was no open space near her car, so I wheeled the truck around toward the back of the lot, where there were a lot fewer cars. A minute later, we were parked and heading into the main entrance of the hospital.

Inside, it was busy, but quiet in the way only hospitals and funeral homes are. The lobby waiting room was sparsely populated, and we were able to approach the main desk without waiting in a line. The woman at the desk – a severe-looking, gray-haired woman who looked as though she had never smiled in her life – stared expectantly at us as we approached.

"We're here to see Helena Abbott. She was admitted last night," I heard myself say.

The woman's face became very mildly irritated. "One moment," she answered, and then added, "this new computerized admissions system gives me fits."

"I'm sorry," Stephanie said.

"Nothing to be sorry about. It's the march of progress," she replied, sounding anything but convinced of the merits of technical advancement. She tapped on her keyboard several times, then made an odd noise that took several seconds for me to recognize as satisfaction. "Eventually I'll get the hang of this thing." She looked up at us, slightly less severe than before. "She's out of intensive care, in room 207. You'll need to check in at the desk upstairs, since there may be a limit on visitors. The elevator's to your left, past the lobby," she added, nodding in that direction.

"Thank you," Steve answered her. We filed out of the lobby into a corridor that led toward the hospital cafeteria; the elevators were on either side as we left the waiting area. One had just opened, disgorging a harried-looking woman some ten years older than we were, along with a kindergarten-age child with a new-looking cast on his right arm. He grinned up at us as he passed, waving the cast so that we could see it.

"Come on, Sammy," his mother said, pulling him past us. Steve grinned as we entered the unusually-large elevator. It could easily hold a hospital gurney and had doors on either side. Stephanie pressed the button for the second floor, and fifteen seconds later, we emerged into a smaller, less open waiting area than the one we had just left. The nurse on duty looked up as we approached.

"Name?" she asked.

"Helena Abbott, room 207," Stephanie answered.

"Ah." She consulted a clipboard briefly. "She has visitors right now. Are you friends or family?"

"Friends," I answered. "We know who's visiting her – her great-niece and her sister. They know we're coming."

She nodded. "I'll call over and let them know you're here." She paused. "Ms. Abbott is in a coma, if you weren't aware of that."

"We know," Stephanie said.

The duty nurse nodded again. We found the sign that indicated which hallway to take. Some sixty feet from the desk, we came to room 207. The door was ajar, and inside, we could see a semi-private room with an empty bed and a drawn curtain behind it. Nana was talking to someone as Steve knocked quietly on the door.

A moment later, Janie came out from behind the curtain. She was calm, but a telltale redness in her eyes betrayed her grief, and she hugged me close, swaying a little. Steve and Stephanie sidled past us into the room. "Hello, Nana," I heard Stephanie say.

"Hello, children," Nana replied quietly. The calm in her voice reminded me that she had been through terrible losses in her life, and that Helena would just be one more. "Thank you for coming."

"We didn't want you to have to be alone," Stephanie answered.

"That's very kind of you," Nana answered. "And I'm glad you cared enough to be here. Lots of kids your age are too selfish these days." She paused. "I'm glad my Janie has friends like you."

"We're glad we got to meet you both," Steve said. Janie looked up at me.

"I'm so glad you're here," she whispered, She was about to kiss me, but Nana's voice drifted from behind the curtain: "Janie! Quit kissing that boy and come back here."

Janie rolled her eyes a little, but she managed a smile, and I had to smile back. "Coming, Nana," she said, and disengaging from me, she took my hand and led me back to where the others were gathered around Helena's bed.

Seeing her was a shock, and not a pleasant one. Helena lay insensate, her back raised, with a tube up her nose and an IV hooked to the back of her hand. Several sensors ran from under her hospital johnny to monitors on the wall behind her bed. Stephanie was holding her free hand, looking sadly down at her.

"The people at New Star did all they could," Janie said, her voice fragile. "They got her here in something like fifteen minutes, and the doctors here were able to stabilize her enough to put her in a coma, but they don't know if she'll recover at all. If she doesn't wake up by tomorrow, we might – we might have to –" she bowed her head, gulping, and then continued, "we might have to turn off the machines and let her go."

"I'm sorry, Janie," I said. "And Nana," I added, looking at her. She was calm, and looked sad and resigned. I realized all over again that without Helena, Nana would have no one left but Janie – and that Janie would have to stay close to Toccoa to take care of her.

Steve had been studying her vital signs in the monitors. "Her blood pressure's a hundred over sixty," he said, frowning. "That's low. Too low. Her pulse is near a hundred, too." He paused. "That can't be good."

"It isn't," Nana said. "She could have another attack if she destabilizes, and I don't think they could save her if that happens." She looked carefully at her granddaughter, and then at the three of us. "Janie, why don't you take your friends to the cafeteria and get something to eat? They've been driving all morning. I'll stay with Helena."

"I don't want to leave, Nana," Janie protested. "What if she wakes up?"

Nana looked reprovingly at her. "We both know that she's stable. It'll take her some time to wake up, if she's going to. Go on, now."

As we filed out, I put my arm around Janie and side-hugged her as she leaned toward me. We followed the corridor for a little while, until Steve halted so suddenly that Stephanie nearly lost her balance – she had been leaning on him as well – and looked at me.

"Mr. Abbott said he was walking here. He doesn't have to follow the roads – I remember that Sarah didn't, either. So he could have come straight across country until he got to I-85, and followed it from there." He looked from me to Stephanie. "If it's ninety miles, and he walks four miles an hour – and he probably can – then he would get here in about a day."

"Then he could get here any minute," Stephanie breathed.

"There's one thing I need to do first," Janie said. "I need to tell my parents what's happening. Helena might be coming to join them soon." She sagged a little as she said this, and I hugged her again briefly.

"Then let's go, now," I whispered.

FIVE MINUTES LATER, we were all piled into Janie's car, driving the half-mile back to the cemetery. It was a sharp turn in from the street, but Janie trundled the huge car smoothly into the cemetery path, going slowly up the hill that hid her parents' resting place from the street.

As the car topped the rise and went slowly downhill, Stephanie gasped and pointed. There were three pale figures standing at the marker. I recognized Janie's parents at once from their clothing, and knew at once who the third one was.

As Janie parked her car some thirty feet from the marker, the three all looked toward us, all waving. Janie's parents were smiling broadly, and even Mr. Abbott seemed glad to see us.

"Albert told us about meeting you," Pastor Sawyer said. "He also told us what happened to my aunt."

"I'm sorry, sir," Stephanie said. "We came back here as soon as we could. Janie called yesterday to tell us."

"Thank you for coming up here," Mrs. Sawyer replied.

Janie was holding my hand, and staring at Mr. Abbott in an odd, happily surprised amazement. "You're my uncle Albert," she whispered. "Aunt Helena told me a lot about you."

"I never knew about you," he said, and motioned toward Steve and Stephanie. "Those two and this boy you're with were the first people in ages to notice that Helena and I ever lived in McDowell Mills." He paused, and then looked toward us with a look of gratitude that I don't think could have been replicated on a human face. "They told me where she is, and what happened to Edward." He paused. "I hadn't met Roberta. Edward was still in grade school when Helena moved here. I can't ever thank you enough for making it possible for me to see them."

"We have to get back to the hospital soon," Janie said. "Nana's sitting with Aunt Helena, but I don't want to be away for long."

Mr. Abbott looked to Janie's parents. "Would you be willing to come with me? Since they can see us, they might be able to get a message to your mother if she awakens." He paused. "That's one of the reasons I'm here."

He glanced toward Janie as he said this, and I realized that he had wanted to see not only Helena, but Nana and Janie as well. He had missed Janie's whole life, and almost half of his sister's.

The Sawyers smiled. "We will come with you to the hospital. It's not time for us to go yet, but I believe it's almost time for you and Helena," Mrs. Sawyer said gently.

"Thank you." Mr. Abbott looked at Janie. "Go ahead and drive back to the hospital. We'll be along soon enough."

As we returned to Janie's car, we could see the three ghosts making their way across the graveyard toward the road. Steve saw me watching them, and said, "They'll be there in a few minutes. Let's get on back."

WE RETURNED TO bedlam. Nana was standing outside the door to Helena's room, her hands over her mouth, looking terribly distressed. We could hear the beeping of monitors and voices speaking urgently inside the room as she looked toward us.

"She crashed," she told us quietly, her voice very slightly unsteady. "It was just a minute or two ago. I'm so sorry." Her face crumpled, and she bowed her head as Janie put her arms around her.

"It's all right, Nana," she whispered. "There wasn't anything you could have done."

Stephanie had put her arms around Steve, who was watching me. We were both listening, trying to hear what was going on in the room. Some of the more strident alarms had stopped, and the voices had calmed somewhat, but I could tell we both had a sense that whatever had happened was too severe for her to overcome.

We stood outside, waiting for what seemed like hours, but was in fact only a few minutes. After a voice called a code over the intercom, two masked staffers left the room without acknowledging us. A few seconds after that, a white-coated, middle-aged man who was clearly an on-duty doctor came out, removing his mask as he looked at us in turn.

"I'll be back here in a few minutes," he said, and then focused on Nana. "I'm afraid your sister's condition has deteriorated. She's had another cardiac arrest, and though she's back with us, I don't expect her to last much longer. These episodes will recur until she can no longer recover. Do you understand?"

Something hardened just a little in Nana's expression as she took this in. "Yes. I understand. How long do you think it will be?"

The doctor paused. "I don't think she'll make it to sundown," he said. "If she lives through the night, we can re-evaluate, but at this point, her prognosis is very poor. You will want to consider end-of-life decisions."

"I already have," Nana said, determined in spite of her emotional state. "She would not want to go on living if she could not see her family. She told me so, not very long ago."

Janie stared at her. "When did she tell you this?" she asked.

"Not long after your friends came up to speak to her this weekend," Nana answered. "We talked on the phone. She said she felt as though their coming meant that Albert would be coming to take her home soon."

In spite of ourselves, the four of us – Janie included – all looked at each other. Steve was the first to speak.

"We need to be in there with her, then. It could be any minute," he said. Janie's eyes widened as she glanced toward him, then at me.

"Come on, Nana," she whispered, leading her back into the room and past the dividing curtain. Steve, Stephanie and I followed. Helena was clearly the worse for the second attack; she was on a respirator, her pulse was higher, and her blood pressure – which had been low before – had increased to 190 over 110.

We surrounded her bed, with Nana sitting and Janie standing on the side near the window, and Steve and Stephanie beside the curtain. I stood next to Janie, at the corner at the bed, glancing at the doorway every few seconds, knowing what was to come.

I hadn't known how long I expected to wait, but it took less time than I had thought it would – maybe three or four slow, quiet minutes punctuated only by the noises from Helena's respirator and vital monitors – before Albert looked into the room from the corridor. Seeing me, he smiled, and walked toward us as Pastor and Mrs. Sawyer came in behind him.

I sidled closer to Janie, nudging her gently with my elbow. Tears sprang in her eyes as she saw the three ghosts come and stand at the foot of the bed, watching Helena with a kindness and tenderness that I suspected only a ghost awaiting reunion could express. There was no sadness in their expressions, and no pity for her suffering.

"Janie, what are you looking at?" Nana suddenly asked in a low voice. She followed Janie's gaze, and mine and our friends, but clearly could see nothing.

"Nana, remember how I could see my mama and daddy – you know, when I was a little girl?" I heard Janie ask. Nana's breath caught in her chest.

"I remember," she said quietly. "What do you see now?"

"They're at the foot of the bed right now," Janie said. "Mama's wearing a pretty sundress that doesn't quite fit her, and Daddy –"

Nana cut her off. "I remember," she said, and if anything, she sounded slightly angered. Janie faltered, looking uncertainly at me.

"Nana, he has sandy blonde hair, and hunches forward just a little," I said. "His wife – Roberta – she has brown hair." As I said this, they both smiled at me, and I saw something I hadn't before. "Roberta has a very sweet smile, even though she has one tooth that's crooked."

Nana turned to face me, sheer disbelief replacing her anger. "Are you telling me *you* see them?" she asked.

"Yes," Stephanie answered her softly. "We can see all three of them. So can Janie."

Nana looked so perplexed, so bewildered by this, that it was several seconds before it sank in, and she could ask: "All three of them?"

Steve leaned across the bed toward her, his hands on the side rail. "Yes. Albert is here, as well. We came here because we could see him, back in McDowell Mills. After Helena had her attack, we told him what had happened. He walked all the way here to be near her."

"I don't know what to think about this," Nana whispered. "Janie always said she could see her Mama and Daddy, when she was a little girl, but she hasn't seen them in years."

"I've been visiting them every few days, since I was old enough to walk to the cemetery," Janie told her. "I've always been able to see them. I took Chad and Steve and Stephanie to their graves so that Mama and Daddy could see them, and that's how we found out they could see them, too."

Nana's eyes were fixed on a point somewhere near where Helena's knees lay beneath her hospital sheet, but she wasn't seeing anything. I looked at each of the others, but when I looked toward Albert, I realized he was watching me, and his expression was one of excited expectation as he nodded toward me.

I moved my hand from Janie's shoulder to Nana's, and she looked up at me. "It's almost time," I whispered. "Albert knows it's almost time."

Nana's hands flew to her mouth again, her eyes snapping shut as her head bowed. Even as I squeezed her shoulder as comfortingly as I could, two of the wall monitors started going off again. Nana's eyes opened again, a tear trickling from each of her eyes, and said softly, "turn them off. Please."

Steve reached over to the monitors, pulling out the cords that connected them to the electrodes on her body. Helena trembled briefly, her eyes fluttering, and was still again. A moment later, two nurses came in, looking suspiciously at Steve, who still held the cords in his hand.

"I told him to," Nana said, her voice breaking. "It was time. Time to let her go."

One of the nurses - a stout, matronly woman in her fifties, holding a clipboard, who looked exactly like the nurse she was – glanced toward the cords. "You only disconnected the monitors, not the respirator," she said, motioning toward the facepiece Helena still wore. She was no longer breathing.

"Yes," Steve answered. "Nana didn't want the noise. She wanted her to go peacefully."

"You have power of attorney?" the nurse asked.

"Yes," Nana answered. The nurse nodded, then said, "I'm sorry for your loss, Mrs. – Sawyer," she said, glancing at her clipboard. "There will be some paperwork to complete, when you are able."

"Of course," Nana answered. "Could I ask that we be left in peace for a few minutes?"

"Yes, ma'am." The other nurse turned to leave. The one with the clipboard started to pull Steve and Stephanie out with her.

"They can stay," Janie and Nana said together. The nurse looked at them, then nodded, released them, and left.

Nana's face began to crumple again, and she leaned forward in her seat. Janie bent to put her arm around her, and the rest of us stood with heads bowed, until a familiar, if windy, voice sounded. "Now, you children should know not to be so upset."

All of us – including Nana – started, and looked toward the foot of the bed. A fourth ghost had joined the three, a woman who had regained the full comeliness that age had almost erased, with blonde, full hair where there had been thin, graying strands before. She wore a dress that had probably been in style during the Second World War, and she was beaming at us, while her husband – Albert – was smiling as well, his arm around her shoulder.

Nana gasped, looking first at her brother and sister-in-law, then to each of the rest of us. "My land!" she managed to utter, and then she saw who was standing behind the Abbotts.

"Edward?" she whispered, her eyes widening, her cheeks tear-streaked. "Bertie?"

They didn't speak, but simply smiled and waved at her. Albert reached over and squeezed his nephew's shoulder, receiving a smile and a nod in return, before he and Roberta turned and walked out of the room, fading as they did.

"No! Wait!" Nana cried. Janie knelt next to her, putting an arm around her.

"It's all right, Jane," Albert said in his warm, musical voice. "They'll be here until it's time for Janie to go, and that might be a while yet."

Nana's eyes were streaming, but she was smiling through them toward Albert and Helena. "They really knew. They brought you back together."

Albert motioned toward each of us. "There's always been a few of the teenagers who could see us," he said. "Usually the younger ones can't, and the adults – even the ones who could see us before then – they often forget," he said quietly. "The ones like us –" he glanced lovingly toward Helena, receiving an equally adoring look in return – "we don't usually talk with the living. Usually they just forget about us. If these three hadn't taken an interest, I don't know how long I would have waited before moving on."

"Moving on?" Nana whispered.

"Yes," Helena said quietly. Even as she said this, we could see a light shining through the curtain dividing the room. It was coming from the hallway, and was growing steadily brighter. Both ghosts looked briefly toward it, then back at us. "It's time for us. We were meant to go together."

Albert nodded. Stephanie's cheeks were as tear-streaked as Nana's, but Janie was smiling bravely. Steve and I looked at each other, and I felt, overwhelmingly, that we had just done something very, very good. I lifted my hand, and waved to Albert and Helena, and quietly said, "Goodbye."

"Goodbye," Steve echoed, and Stephanie whispered, "Goodbye, Mr. Abbott. Goodbye, Helena."

They smiled at us all one final time, and turned, and moved beyond the curtain. For a moment, they shaded the light beyond it as they went into the hallway, but as that light began to fade, we could hear a last, distant call: "Thank you!"

CHAPTER EIGHT

THE THREE OF US ended up spending the night at Nana's house, in part because of what had happened, but also because Janie had said there was one more place she wanted us to see before we went back to our homes.

"Toccoa Falls is named for a real waterfall," she told us. Steve nodded agreement as she continued, "and it was where the water from the dam break came down onto the college. I'd like for you to go there with me. I've never seen any ghosts there, but I've had a feeling about the place since I was a little girl, and I'd like to know whether you all can sense anything about it."

We agreed, and by ten that morning, we were riding in Janie's huge Oldsmobile back past the cemetery. Stephanie had asked Janie whether she wanted to stop there, but she had demurred. "You need to get back home today," she said, looking wistfully at me. "I don't want your folks to stop letting you come up here."

"I think it'll be OK," I answered. We had each called our families the previous evening; my Mom had been fine with my staying, but had insisted on speaking briefly with Nana to ensure proper decorum would be observed. Stephanie's mother had had similar reservations, but three minutes' conversation was enough to allay her concerns.

We all felt slightly unclean, wearing the same clothes we'd come up in the day before, but we knew we'd be home by midafternoon, so it wasn't too terrible. Janie drove us past the hospital onto the college campus, following Forrest Drive through the small community until the road ended at a cottage and gift shop, with a small parking lot across the street. She parked, and we got out, looking along the path that led up from the cottage into the hillside forest beyond it.

"The falls are a little less than a quarter mile through those trees," Janie said. "When the flood came, it went right over the waterfall."

"Do you come here a lot?" Steve asked. He was hiding it well, but I could tell he was slightly apprehensive. Stephanie could see it also, and leaned close to him as we began to walk toward the trail.

"Nana and I used to come up here about once a year," Janie answered. "Nana always did it to remember Mama and Daddy. We would have a picnic and watch the waterfall. It was always quiet up there."

"Quiet," Steve said softly. He looked at me. "Remember what I told you, about that graveyard in Savannah?"

I thought about that for a few seconds as we walked, and all at once, I understood what he meant, and why he felt hesitant about going up to the falls.

"Whoa," Stephanie breathed, and I realized she felt it, too. I looked toward Janie. She was walking straight ahead, her eyes on the path, her face blank except for a hint of solemnity.

"Janie, what's up here?" I whispered. "What is it you haven't told us?"

She slowed her pace, but didn't stop, and her eyes closed for a few seconds. Her hand found mine and squeezed it tightly before she looked toward me again.

"I don't really know," she answered. "It's not evil, and it's not a ghost like Mama and Daddy. It's something else, something really – really –" Her voice trailed off.

"Really *old*," Steve finished for her. Janie looked toward him.

"That's it," she said. "Whatever is here, has been here for centuries, or longer. It was here before anyone from Europe ever came to America."

"This is its home," Steve added. "And people like us have started moving in, and changing things. We created the Hartwell Reservoir. We built towns, and cleared land. We haven't coexisted with it."

"And it will be here after we go away," I added. For a moment I could see trees, huge trees, bigger than any that had ever been in this forest, and a feeling of an incredible distance. "It's ancient. It's as ancient as the mountains." I looked toward Janie again.

"Whatever this is, it's not even thousands of years old. It's millions. And it's huge," I whispered.

Janie nodded to me, and then added, "I know. But it never frightened me. I've always felt as though it was grieving, but I don't know why."

We continued toward the falls with increasing trepidation. Whatever the presence was, it didn't seem to grow stronger; it was much larger than just the waterfall, or even the town that nestled below it. Its center felt far to the north, well into the mountains where few people lived.

We reached the pool at the base of the waterfall, and halted. It was surprisingly small; if it had been a parking lot, six cars wouldn't have fit in it. The falls themselves were a little taller than I expected, cascading down a rocky cliff in a white sheet with a small penumbra of mist where they met the pool. I remembered what Steve had said – the flood had been caused by a dam break above the falls – and shuddered.

Steve looked as unsettled as I felt. "I read that when the dam broke, the water coming over the falls was at a tenth the rate of the Mississippi River," he said quietly. "The Mississippi is a mile wide. This is barely twenty yards across." He looked up. "It must have been thirty feet high before it got to the falls. Coming in the middle of the night like that –" he paused. We all, Janie included, looked fearfully around ourselves.

The waterfall's gentle roar had masked it, but we could just hear the rush of the great wall of water, not only as it came over the falls, but echoing off the hills above them, where the dam had broken. I closed my eyes, and all at once I could see it – a moonless, rainy night, with the overflow from the dam running downhill to the falls, and a sound that could only have been the first groanings of the earth as the dam – built, then neglected (*like all things made by the white man!*) – strained, shifted, and all at once gave way.

I opened my eyes again. We were all staring at each other.

"It didn't want to hurt anyone," I said softly. "The people who built the dam didn't take care of it."

"It was grieving for the people who died," Steve added. He glanced toward Janie. "It knew your parents died. It still knows. All it wants is the quiet."

"Like in that graveyard," I put in. Both girls looked at me.

"I told Chad about it when we were riding around Lavonia," Steve said. He related his experience with the old Savannah cemetery, concluding, "this really feels a lot like that. It's not evil, and it's not malevolent. It doesn't want to hurt anything or anyone. It just wants quiet."

Almost as if we had heard the thing say so, we all fell silent again, listening to the falls, and to the echoes of a past, distant tragedy.

AN HOUR LATER, we were back at Nana's, saying our goodbyes. Nana insisted on hugs from each of us, and planted a kiss on my cheek. Janie was grinning at me, but Nana only told us, "you don't know how much your visits have meant to me. Thank you for everything."

"As soon as we know when and where the funeral will be, I'll call you," Janie told me. I nodded. "We're going to try to make it Saturday or Sunday, since school starts here on Monday."

"It starts for us, too," Stephanie said.

"Senior year," I said. "One more year until we can get out of McDowell Mills."

Stephanie and Steve got in the truck as Janie approached me. She hugged me close with a kiss, and murmured, "I know you wouldn't want to go to the college here."

"I'm already looking at going to Clemson," I murmured back.

Those were the magic words. She kissed me again, much more energetically, and for a few seconds I didn't think about anything else.

Stephanie, however, must have decided that since she couldn't imitate Mr. Singer, she would go for the closest thing available: she laid on the horn for about five seconds, completely disrupting the mood. Steve was laughing, no doubt remembering the bowling alley in Jackson Creek again, and I had to chuckle myself. Janie grabbed my shoulders before I could turn to get in the truck.

"I'll call you as soon as I know about the funeral," she whispered. "Thank you for everything."

I smiled back at her. "No need to thank me. Meeting you was better than anything I could have hoped for."

She kissed me again, and then let me get in the truck. I expected a round of hazing from Stephanie and Steve, but they were quiet, and as I drove the truck back out onto Big A Road toward Lavonia, I looked toward them for a moment.

"She's the real thing, isn't she?" Stephanie asked.

I didn't even have to think about it. "Yeah. She is. And she's one of us."

Steve laughed a little at this. It's going to be fun for you, trying to go back and forth during senior year."

"We'll make it work," I heard myself say. I was already starting to wonder how life at Clemson would be – would I stay on campus, up in the mountains? Would Janie be able to get in, and would she live there – or would she live with Nana, and commute?

These thoughts occupied me as I drove the truck back into Lavonia, then onto I-85, southward toward home.

JANIE CALLED ME the next day with some interesting, and unexpected, news. "Nana decided against a funeral service," she told me. "Aunt Helena asked in her will to be cremated, and her ashes scattered at the falls. Nana wants for you and Steve and Stephanie to come back on Saturday, if you can."

"I think that'll be all right," I replied. I'd already mentioned to my mother that Helena had passed, so I was already fairly sure I could go.

"Aunt Helena left me her car, and most of her savings," she said. "It'll be enough for me to go to Clemson, if that's what you decide."

Thankfully, Mom was in the living room, but I lowered my voice to be safe. "I'd like to. Are you sure? I mean, what if spring rolls around and you decide I'm too boring for you?"

I hadn't said so, but she was so pretty, and the changes in her life were enough that I wondered whether the boys at her high school would notice them – and her.

"I doubt that," she answered, laughing a little, but then continuing more soberly. "You and Steve and Stephanie changed my life. Without you, Nana wouldn't have seen Mama and Daddy again. Helena and Albert wouldn't have gotten to leave together." She paused. "And I wouldn't have any of you as friends. Or –" She abruptly stopped speaking.

"Or what?" I asked. I hoped I knew the answer.

"Or you as my boyfriend," she answered at last. "I've never had one before, not even when I was little."

"I've had girlfriends before," I said, "but none like you. Not even close."

"Because I could see ghosts, like you?" she asked me. I realized that she was serious. She didn't have a clue.

"That's only a small part of it," I replied, and took a deep breath. "The first time we met at New Star, even though you didn't seem happy to see any of us, all I could think about was how pretty you were, and how I hoped you wouldn't just kick us out, because I wanted to get to know you better."

"Really? You think I'm pretty?" She seemed genuinely surprised. Even if she wasn't, I knew it was time.

"Janie, you're not just pretty. You're beautiful. I don't think I would have forgotten you even if you'd kicked us all out," I said, my voice shaking slightly. "I've never seen anyone or met anyone like you." I swallowed, and then managed to say, "I love you."

I could hear her breathe, a little unevenly, through the line. A few seconds passed, and then she said, in a voice as broken as mine, "I never thought I would hear someone say that to me. I didn't know if I would ever get to say that to someone else. But I always hoped," she said, taking a deep breath of her own, "and I love you, too."

I was a little overcome, and unsure of what to say, when my mother came into the kitchen. One look from her and I knew I was going to be grilled about that phone call. "I have to go. I'll let you know as soon as I clear it with my folks. See you Saturday?"

"You'd better," she said. "Bye."

The line clicked dead before I could answer. My mom looked at me appraisingly.

"This girl's special, isn't she?" she inquired. "It's not just that her aunt died."

"Yeah. She's different." I didn't want to go into too many details, so I only said, "the funeral's on Saturday. Nana said it should just be the three of us, her, and Janie, and that we would scatter her ashes at the waterfall in Toccoa."

"Just be back before dark," she said. "And this came in the mail for you." She handed me a thick envelope with a familiar, orange pawprint in the upper left corner. "Be careful with this girl, Chad. You might end up stuck someplace where you don't want to be."

"Have you ever been up in the mountains?" I asked her.

"Not really," she hedged. "Not often. Your dad and I are more beach people."

"Toccoa is right at the edge of the mountains," I said. "I'd like to go to school somewhere like that. I really love it there."

My mom studied me for a few seconds – long enough to make me uncomfortable. "Are you sure it's the place you're in love with, and not who's there?"

"Mom…" I shook my head for a minute. "Look, Janie's special, for sure. But I'd decided to study engineering, and no matter which branch I pick, Clemson's one of the best engineering schools in the country. For chemical engineering, it's *the* best."

"I thought Georgia Tech was pretty good for engineering, too. And you could live at home," Mom said.

I sighed. "Mom, it's not that I don't want to live at home, but if I can swing it, I'd like to be out of McDowell Mills."

"I can understand that," she replied, with a small, rueful smile. "I wouldn't want to be young and stuck here. If you can get a scholarship, or some kind of grant, then I think you should go. Maybe you should call your uncle."

"Uncle Phil?" I asked. Phil was my Dad's younger brother; we didn't have a lot in common, but we had always gotten along well – Phil got along with everyone – and I knew that he would help out if I asked.

"Phil's a Clemson alumnus," Mom said, and grinned at my obvious surprise. "He's also a registrar at Erskine College. That's about 30 miles from Clemson, so you could visit him sometimes." Her smile took on a hint of reproval. "If you're not too busy."

"I'll make time," I said at once. Just knowing that I might not only be going there, but could get help in paying for it, had me really excited. Until then, I'd resigned myself to staying in McDowell Mills until I graduated, but suddenly I was looking at the possibility of escaping four years early.

ON SATURDAY MORNING, I picked up Stephanie, and drove up to meet Steve in Tuckerton. Stephanie didn't talk much along the way, and I realized that though we knew we shouldn't date, and were still friends, she was still slightly uncomfortable about Janie. I hoped she got over it quickly, since I really wanted for all four of us to remain close.

Her unease subsided the moment Steve hopped into the truck for the drive to Toccoa, but she still leaned against him for most of the drive. I told them about my decision to apply at

Clemson, and about my uncle; both of them responded positively, especially Steve.

"This works out for you almost as well as things did for me, with Uncle Fred," he told me as we passed Braselton. "You can escape McDowell Mills, go to college with Janie, and maybe find out more about whatever it is that's up there." He seemed a bit less enthusiastic about that last part, and over the next few miles, something occurred to me.

"Steve, you said you felt that sort of longing for quiet in the cemetery in Savannah, and again at the falls," I commented. "One thing I'm curious about – did they feel sort of the same, or did they feel exactly the same? Was it two similar things, or were they identical?"

Steve hesitated, then thought about this for some time. I don't know whether this had occurred to him; knowing Steve, I thought he had considered this already, but didn't have a good answer.

"I don't think they're the same," he said at last. "I mean, both places have that sort of ancient, timeless feel to them, but not in the same way. The one in Savannah was gentler." He thought about it, then suddenly snapped his fingers, making Stephanie jump slightly in surprise.

"There was a river that bordered the cemetery in Savannah," he said. "It's the river that separates the mainland from the islands – the coastal waterway. I can't remember the name. But it's really calm, and winds around the islands and marshes." I glanced toward him; he was staring out the windshield, deep in thought. "The difference was in the water. The waterfall in Toccoa is fresher, and cold, and just starting toward the ocean. It's more energetic," he continued.

Stephanie had roused herself as Steve spoke. "And the water near the ocean is at the end of its journey," she said. "It's slower, and older in its cycle. It's almost always peaceful, like it's sleeping, unless there's a storm."

I was getting drawn into this as well. "And water in Toccoa is fast, but it doesn't have the power it has nearer the sea," I said. "Not unless…" My voice trailed away, and we all reached the same conclusion at once.

"The dam break," I said.

"And the baby carried on the water," Steve added. "I wonder if the water – or whatever is connected with it – knew. I wonder if it knows about us."

We were all silent for several miles, and finally, as we passed the exit to Carnesville, some ten miles from the Lavonia exit, I said, "I guess when we get there, we'll find out."

WE REACHED NANA'S house some forty minutes later. Since Nana had decided that we should have a ceremony with just the five of us, Janie had asked us to call her when we got to Lavonia, so that we would know to be ready. This we did, calling from the pay phone outside the Waffle Grille. I noticed that Cassandra was working again that day; she looked out the window for a moment, and I could see she was trying to remember who I was, so I finished the call and left as hastily as I could.

I was relieved to see that Nana was dressed in everyday clothes. The three of us hadn't dressed for anything formal, since the funeral was just for us. The six of us – Steve was holding Helena's urn – got into Janie's Oldsmobile, with me in front beside her and Nana in back between Stephanie and Steve. I glanced back toward them for a second, and couldn't help but grin.

"I didn't think anything could come between you two," I observed. Stephanie made a face at me, but Nana gave Steve an appraising look that was so comical that we all started to laugh – including Janie, who watched the exchange in the rearview mirror.

The more or less happy mood prevailed until we reached the little lodge at the base of the path. Janie parked as close to the head of the trail as she could, and we all got out and started along it toward the falls – this time with Nana between me and Janie, just in case she needed support. Steve was still carrying Helena.

"Good grief, Nana, you just can't leave the boys alone, can you?" Steve asked. Nana laughed at this.

"No way I'm going to come between these two," she said, smiling up at each of us. "Am I?"

"Never," Janie said.

"We'll both be here for you," I heard myself answer. Nana took my hand and squeezed it briefly, and we walked the rest of the way to the falls in silence.

At the pool, we fanned out until we all stood at the bank. Steve lifted the cover of the urn, and as he did, a light breeze swirled lazily among the trees at the base of the cliffs where the falls descended. As I looked about to see whether anyone else was present, I was moderately surprised to see two familiar, faint faces approaching on the trail behind us.

Edward and Roberta – Bertie, as Nana had called her – were walking hand in hand up the trail, only a few yards behind us. I nudged Janie, and then whispered to Nana, "there's two more here."

Nana turned, and her eyes lit up as she saw her son again. Janie was smiling as well.

"Hello, Mama. Hi, Daddy," she said quietly. They both waved, and Edward spoke in his windy voice: "Janie told us you would have the funeral here, today. Helena and Albert have gone on, but we can say our goodbyes here."

Steve came alongside Nana, holding the urn; she reached into it, drawing some of Helena's ashes out, and allowed them to slide through her fingers into the breeze, floating out into the pool and drifting onto the cliffs. Janie did likewise, and then Nana motioned toward me.

"I want for all of you to do this with me," she said. "Helena didn't have anyone, except me and Janie, until the very end. You three gave her more than anyone else after the flood took Edward and Bertie." I glanced toward Edward; his smile was faded slightly, but he nodded his approval. "I can never thank you enough, and I know she was more grateful even than I am," she added.

I reached carefully into the urn; the ashes were more than half gone. I took a small handful out and let them scatter through my fingers as Janie and Nana had done.

Stephanie was next, and then Steve poured out the remaining ashes directly from the urn into the pool. Edward and Bertie looked at each of us.

"Part of Helena has already begun to flow toward the sea," Bertie said, motioning toward the stream that lead away from the pool.

"And part of her remains here, for a while," Edward added, motioning toward the cliffs where some of her ashes remained. "But as the days pass, and the rains come, little by little her last presence will flow into the ocean, even as she remains part of the waters that return."

We all fell silent, and through the sound of the waterfall and the wind in the trees, I could hear the echoes again, only amongst them, I could hear Helena's musical laugh, and beneath that, the contented sigh of the water.

EPILOGUE

THREE MONTHS LATER

Thursday, November 18, 1993

I DIALED JANIE'S number, my hands shaking slightly in excitement. The line buzzed three times, seeming to take an hour between each one. I sincerely hoped she was home; I had to be at my job in thirty minutes – I'd taken a dishwashing and cleanup job at Cleve's – and I wanted to tell her the good news right away.

Finally, the line clicked, and Nana's voice came along the line. "Hello?"

"Hi, Nana!" I said, trying to contain myself. "How're you?"

"I'm just fine, dear," she answered. "I was just listening to this album Nirvana released last month. You know, I think these boys need to spend some time up at the Falls. They seem so *tense* about everything."

I was familiar with Nirvana, though I didn't listen to them often; their music was preferred by the more disaffected greasers – the ones smart enough to know they were trapped in

McDowell Mills, unless they could somehow figure a way out. The local adults, of course, loathed the sound of them, and playing their music loudly while driving was as good a way to get ticketed – or worse – by the local police as having a bumper sticker reading "Cops are Wusses."

"They are that," I observed. I heard Nana snort.

"I know, you're more into that alternative stuff. I imagine you want to talk with Janie?" she asked.

"Yes, please, ma'am." I replied.

"Oh, all right, then. You'd better be back up here soon to see us." She muffled the phone with her hand, but I could still hear her calling Janie. I waited, feeling like I would explode with my news.

"Hi, Chad!" Janie said. "What's up?"

Janie and I had agreed that I would call one weekend, then drive up the other weekend. That way, I could keep from having expenses pile up too high when I was having to save everything I could for college. Calling on a Thursday was definitely not in the plan, so she knew something important had happened.

"I got into Clemson," I said, "and my uncle was able to get me an alumni scholarship. It means I have in-state tuition and pays half my tuition costs."

"Awesome!" Janie cried. "So you're definitely going?"

"Definitely," I said. "And I got a call from Steve yesterday. He says he's found something strange in Tuckerton, and we may have to check that out, too."

"Really?" she asked. "What'd he find?"

"There's a cemetery near Tuckerton that's really weird," I answered. "He hasn't seen anything there yet, but the way the place feels is really strange." I paused. "Not in a good way. It's a Civil War-era graveyard near Tuckerton, where one of the battles took place. He said it felt – 'ominous,' was the word he used."

"Is there, like, a river or lake near it?" she asked.

"That's the thing," I said, remembering what Steve had told me. "There's no water nearby. And he noticed something else, too, when he was looking on a map of Stone Mountain. The town, not the mountain."

"What was it?" Janie asked.

"He was wondering whether the stream from Toccoa Falls led down through Tuckerton, or if it was in the same basin," I said. "It doesn't, obviously – that flows into Lake Hartwell, and goes from there down to Savannah. But this cemetery is less than a mile from where two different creeks rise. One eventually flows into the Atlantic Ocean in Brunswick, through the Altamaha River, and the other flows into the Chattahoochee, and empties into the Gulf of Mexico."

"Whoa," Janie said. "That's amazing."

"It's called the Continental Divide," I continued. "It runs right through Tuckerton, Stone Mountain and Atlanta. North and west of it, everything flows to the Gulf, and everything south and east goes into the Atlantic."

We had talked at length about the water spirit at the Falls, and what it might mean. What Steve had described promised something strange indeed, and the history of the place made it even more concerning.

Janie had caught on quickly. "So you potentially have two different water streams in a place where a Civil War battle was fought. That sounds bad."

"From what he says, it was." I paused. "I was going to ask whether you'd like to meet in Tuckerton next weekend, and visit Steve," I said. "If it's OK with Nana."

"I'll ask her," Janie said, and then lowered her voice. "But I think I should wait until tomorrow to ask, if that's all right."

"That's fine," I said. "I'll call you this time tomorrow, then."

"OK." She paused for a moment. "I'm really excited that you're going to be at Clemson. I put in an application there, but I haven't heard back yet."

"So am I," I answered. "Love you."

"Love you too," she answered, and the line went dead. I replaced the receiver, looking forward to a few minutes' call with her the next day, a weekend with her and my friends in Tuckerton – a place I'd never spent much time in – and, down the road, the chance to spend a lot more time together with her, going to school in the mountains I'd come to love.

ABOUT THE AUTHOR

M. C. Vaughn is a retired industrial engineering generalist/data analyst turned fantasy and science fiction author. Toccoa's Echoes is his fifth book and the second in the Salem's Ghosts series. He lives with his family in Savannah, Ga.

<u>The Legends of Starreach Realm</u>:
Monolith (Book One)
Sanctum (Book Two – coming in 2025)

<u>Phoebe</u>:
Phoebe
The Gray Angel

<u>Salem's Ghosts</u>:
Salem's Ghosts
Toccoa's Echoes